Clueless
in SEATTLE

by
Steve Oliver

Off By One
Press

ISBN 0-964413-6-8
Library of Congress Catalog Card Number: 94-92456

All of the events and characters
depicted in this book are fictional.

Illustrations by the author.

Contents

CLUELESS IN SEATTLE

For Simon there had been no magic. All he got out of his trip to the Empire State Building were boring post-cards and an enormous Visa bill.

He had married, but not because he found someone wonderful. He had married because all his friends were getting married.

And he wasn't alone now because of the tragic death of his spouse. He was alone because he and his ex-wife had finally gotten to know each other.

Simon vowed to remain alone until he found the right woman, one who would provide that which had been denied him in youth—intelligent company.

The son of a factory worker, Simon sought a higher intellectual and social plane. As a young man he took a degree in liberal arts because he felt it was a path to society's current royalty—the intellectual—the person of knowledge and taste. He had attended a small, but intellectually snotty state college and graduated with honors, yet he often lied to people, telling them he had graduated from Harvard. In the years following graduation he had become an English instructor at a junior college, and was hoping for an opening in a university.

He chose his roommates for their intelligence and taste. His most recent roommate, Ellsworth, had been an opera buff majoring in stage design. Simon felt that his own taste would improve simply by his association with Ellsworth. Perhaps he would even meet Miss Right among Ellsworth's friends.

Ellsworth appeared completely happy and flawless as he listened to his prized operatic recordings and shared *Pouilly-fuissé* with his chanteuse girlfriend. He eschewed margarine, American cooking generally, and the decline of good taste caused by television, franchise food, and pedestrian lust.

When Simon was in Ellsworth's company he was careful to say the right things or say nothing—to prevent any exposure of his lapses in taste. After all, despite Simon's aspirations, he had not been raised in grand surroundings. He had lived his childhood in an old clapboard house with linoleum floors and had spent a lot of his time imagining what it would be like to grow up on marble tile and oriental carpets.

He had not yet imagined it accurately.

But even Ellsworth, Simon's guide to a better life, turned out, if not to have feet of clay, to have shoes that had trod a barnyard. Simon returned from work early one evening, came in the back way, and discovered his mentor watching a rerun of *Gilligan's Island* and doing an imitation of Barney Fife being tickled. Mid-giggle Ellsworth noticed Simon in the doorway and snapped the remote control with such vigor he probably added velocity to the airborne photons. He changed the station to PBS, but through a miscalculation of the time of day they were suddenly faced by Mister Rogers singing a welcome to his neighborhood. He clicked the instrument off and pretended to be perusing an issue of *Opera News*.

Simon wondered about Ellsworth's behavior, but it didn't dissuade him from trying to improve his *own* taste and the quality of the company he kept.

He moved out.

Simon continued his pursuit of the better life and the better woman. He bought a used Mercedes, ate Quiche Lorraine, and drank Nicaraguan coffee. He accepted friends carefully, never socialized with co-workers unless they were superiors, and practiced his

J.D. Salinger impersonation for parties.

Then he met Xanthia.

She was the personification of a vision he'd held since graduate school. She was svelte and attractive and had read all the pertinent classics. (He hadn't, but it was still a requirement for his dates—either that or an exceptional GRE score.) She held a special fondness for Dylan Thomas and Theodore Roethke, and Robbe-Grillet was her favorite novelist. She refused to watch English language films, and when she talked in her sleep she muttered lines from Chekhov's better plays (in Russian, of course). He thought surely this was a woman who could not disappoint. (This was also the period when his ancient childhood collection of *Uncle Scrooge* comics and a box of Lucky Charms went into hiding.)

Their moments together were a mutual rejection of the tawdry, the commonplace, and the trite. They attended plays and reviewed them at leisure over Chartreuse at a local nightspot. When they shared a bed, it was a handmade English four-poster Xanthia's grandfather had purchased on a trip abroad during the 1930s.

Finally, he had found the one woman who could make him happy.

Then one night he was sleeping lightly (partly because he enjoyed the awareness of her near him and partly because he had a tendency to drool when he went into REM sleep) when something disturbed him and caused him to open his eyes. His love was not in bed and in fact was not in the room.

He slipped into the satin brocade robe he had bought for the nights he spent with her and wandered sleepily through the halls of her apartment, expecting that perhaps it had occurred to her that she didn't know the correct spelling for Balthazar and had gone to look it up, or was on some equally erudite mission.

But the living room was empty, as were the bathroom and kitchen. Then he noticed a little light escaping from the hall closet. That seemed odd, so he opened the door. The Japanese could not have been more shocked to learn that Hirohito was not a god than Simon was to find his Xanthia sitting cross-legged on the closet floor with a *National Enquirer* spread out on her lap. A half-eaten Hostess HoHo protruded obscenely from her lips, though briefly, as she quickly stuffed it into her mouth with sticky, crumb-covered fingers. On the floor beside her was a half-consumed Slurpee. Obviously, she had made a run to the 7-11 down the street.

Then came the inevitable truths. She had lied about her ancestry. She was actually the daughter of an itinerant janitor and part-time book scout and had achieved her education in literature through the accident that it was just about the only reading material in their mobile home—except for the *National Enquirer*. She had worked hard to leave her past behind, but her compulsion for some of the pleasures of her childhood drove her to these midnight revels in trashy food and literature. She promised Simon it was an obsession she could overcome with his support, and after cleaning her up and burning the remains of her habit in the fireplace, they returned to bed. Neither of them slept well that night. For his part he was wondering about the headline he had read in her *National Enquirer* before he burned it.

The relationship resumed, but with a predictable amount of suspicion added. Several times he caught her hurriedly burning items in the fireplace when he arrived for a visit. Once, the top item looked suspiciously like *Soap Opera Digest.* He found a flyer from K-Mart stuck under the Cuisinart and Slim Whitman records behind the stereo. The end came when she made him a soufflé in which she had accidentally included several candy bars and a Pudding Pop.

The end of the relationship was hard on Xanthia. (It probably didn't help that he sent her a subscription to *Official Detective* for her birthday.) Soon afterward she dropped out of law school, sublet her apartment, and started walking the streets collecting shopping bags. Her taste was not completely gone—she only accepted de-signer label bags.

Simon also passed through many changes. He lost contact with friends and tried to join a motorcycle club. This didn't last long, as he was blackballed for coming to a meeting on a Honda Elite and carrying a bottle of sparkling cider to drink at the bonfire. After that he joined a book club as a substitute for the biker life. And he continued to reexamine his values.

But no existential crisis could stop the inevitable buildup of hormonal pressure, and Simon soon began looking at the third finger of the left hand of every attractive woman he met. He started wondering what it would be like to be married to Julia Roberts. In time, he even began wondering where Xanthia had gone. Xanthia had been very close to his ideal. Perhaps he should have stayed with her. In desperation he visited the last place she had been seen but found only a few substandard shopping bags and junk food wrappers.

He gave up on locating Xanthia and resumed dreams about Julia Roberts, but before he could become really morose he met a new woman.

Her name was Petrina. She was from Russia and had been a full professor in her last position at a university. He was fascinated from the start and wondered if her family was secretly descended from royalty—or, even better, from a member of the Central Committee. In some ways it didn't matter if she was descended from either group since, as a former citizen of a former Soviet state, Petrina represented a special kind of royalty. Simon was a liberal and a college instructor after all, and he longed for a more perfect society, one in which success was mandated rather than left to the rough and tumble of competition with less intelligent, but often tougher and more brutal, competitors. Petrina had lived in a society that he imagined represented such idealistic realities. Even though communism was somewhat discredited now, he thought that much of the criticism it received was undeserved, and although there had been some economic difficulties, it still represented a purer way for those of intelligence to foster order and clarity. Petrina had lived in such a pure climate all her life and was therefore unsullied by any possible lust for Grand Slam breakfasts, shopping at Nordstrom, or making a fortune by running an espresso cart franchise.

He had met Petrina at a reading of Russian authors at a local bookstore. They had both laughed at the way the master of ceremonies had mispronounced authors' names and several Russian words. (Simon knew about such things because he had studied Russian history during the period when it was assumed that Marxism would soon be adopted in the United States.) They later had tea at a cafe run by a Russian expatriate, then had a second date at the opera. By the time of the second date Simon had declared—to himself—his love for Petrina. During his lectures at the junior college, he now day-dreamed about her—instead of the coed in the front row whose short skirts seemed to insist that he inspect the inner area of her upper thigh.

Petrina would help to define his life as that of an intellectual. They would have a large house, perhaps similar to the *dachas* so popular with the Party aristocracy when they were in power. Naturally, he would use her as a guide on how to behave in intellectual circles. Unlike his own childhood, her upbringing had been authentic, a proper background for one who desired the life of museums, art galleries, and the pursuit of political truths. Her father was a professor, her mother a chemist. Her own education had focused on classical Russian literature—minus those volumes purged as being philosophically corrupt. Her taste in music and art was also superb, without any corrupting influence from the West. Her desire to listen to classical music was as natural as breathing. With Americans it was so often forced, as you might expect in a country in which the largest audience for classical music was people riding elevators.

But at the very apex of his infatuation, in only their third meeting, Simon discovered a fatal flaw in Petrina. It seemed his fate to suffer disappointment at the hands of near-perfect women.

It was during their discussion of the symphony they had just seen that Petrina began an uncharacteristic outburst.

"Why is it that you always want to beat this horse 'til it has expired?" she asked, leaving Simon to deal with her idiom. "You always want to talk, talk, talk about the music, or the book—as though you had written it, or as though you were a musician. It's just music. It was nice, but can't we talk about something else?"

Simon pushed back in his chair, nearly spilling his

double-tall nonfat latte in the process. Her objection was startling, but he was, of course, willing to accommodate one so much nearer the intellectual center than he.

"I thought you enjoyed talking about music. What else would you like to talk about? We can talk about anything, darling."

"I know, I'm sorry," said Petrina. "I get so mean sometimes I could hit myself with a stick. I just get tired talking about these things. They are like the air—we just breathe it—we don't pull it from our lungs and look at the little particles." She held the invisible little particles in her fingers.

"There are so many things that are more interesting—there are so many things I want to learn now that I live in this country."

"What would you like to learn? I'm sure I could help. I'd like nothing more than to help. What do you want to know?"

"Well," said Petrina, furrowing her brow in that cute, intense Russian way, "I would like to know if it's really possible to buy a house with no down payment. Is it possible?"

Simon sat looking at her for a long time to allow the question to sink in. What did it mean? Why would she want to know this? Scenes from late-night real estate info-mercials forced themselves into his consciousness.

"I'm not sure," he confessed. "I don't know much about real estate. Why do you want to know?"

"I want to make money," she said. "I like the idea of owning property. I want to make a lot of money, and retire—working part-time from my home. I think real estate is the key. That's what I've heard."

Simon was mildly nauseated. "I have to go home," he said suddenly. "I'm not feeling well."

"I'm so sorry," said Petrina. "I'll go with you."

"No, no, I need to go alone."

"I'll talk to you soon," she said, as he left, but Simon knew she would never hear from him again. He would not be able to overcome his aversion to the notion of making money in such a crass way, of associating with such crass people. It had been his secret hope that she knew little or nothing about the ownership of property. In his own dream of owning a *dacha* he had not even considered the practical aspects of such a move. Deep within him was the vague hope that perhaps *dachas* would simply be awarded to college instructors through some enlightened government program.

Petrina tried to contact him, but he avoided her. She continued to phone him until he was forced to tell her about his aversion to her pursuit of real estate. She hung up on him and he returned to his work and quiet life and resumed the daydreams about the girl in the front row.

After a long stretch of boredom Simon determined to try again to locate the woman of his dreams. Since he was enough of a romantic to believe that his mate did exist, it was only a small leap to believe that she lived in this very city. All he had to do was locate her somehow. He decided that his best bet was to try the personals. The more he thought about it the better the idea seemed. He could be *very* specific about his desires—he could pour out his heart into the list of qualities he sought. And, in the tiny part of this plan that required fate, he could be sure that she, his intended, would be in the mood to read the personals when the ad appeared, and would recognize herself.

Being an intelligent and literary person, Simon was very proud of the resulting ad. The only problem was the length—it took more than 700 words to describe him and his needs. He even included snippets of personal history and anecdotes about women who had nearly satisfied his requirements. At first he was worried that Xanthia or Petrina or someone else would recognize themselves through references in the ad, but he finally decided he had disguised them enough.

He paid a hefty sum to run the ad and waited for the results.

At first they were disappointing. Some of the women who responded seemed impressed by his apparent intelligence, but they overestimated their own. Others didn't seem to care what he had said in the ad and seemed to be responding to his ad in a generic way, as perhaps they did to all the ads in the paper.

"You seem like a nice guy," said one letter. "That's

what I'm looking for. I like to go to movies and watch TV."

By the time he was about halfway through the letters he had to go to an office supply store to buy a shredder just to make sure he wouldn't be tempted to reply.

Finally, he received an interesting response. She said she was a professor of Art history who had long sought an intelligent man to share her life. She described herself as beautiful and sensitive, and yet "sensual." There was something about the tone of her writing that seemed familiar, as though he had met her before. Still, unless it had been a meeting in a former life, that could not be. As he read the letter he began to feel he had found the woman who would share his life.

But she had made it difficult for him to share his life with her as she had not provided her name, phone number, or mailing address. Instead, she had suggested that it might be interesting for intelligent people to meet through a game—a series of clues providing a prelude to a sublime introduction. She said she would not make the clues difficult—it would merely be a way to start things off in an interesting manner. This part of the letter moved Simon from dreamy and romantic anticipation to sexual excitement that all but drove the front-row coed from his libido.

She had given a single initial clue—to a location in the city—and promised to provide additional clues at each destination. The first clue was very simple, "The entrance to the ugliest and most poorly managed building in the city." This, of course, was the Kingdome, long the object of his scorn and a frequent subject for his opinions even to friends of short acquaintance. He proceeded to this despicable icon on the appointed evening and when he arrived there found an envelope pasted on a wall. Inside was a small piece of paper with the clue, "An overpriced restaurant with a view to a kill." This, also, was easy to find—a restaurant he could not afford but disliked because he saw it as a gathering spot for the *nouveau riche*, not the tasteful. Like the Kingdome it also was a frequent target of his criticisms. It was located near a bridge that crossed a ravine into which despondent individuals had a habit of leaping. The odd thing about the clue—spooky almost—was that he had often described this restaurant in almost identical terms. This was surely a further sign of their intellectual compatibility.

At the restaurant the parking attendant gave him a note. It read, "Don't jump yet, my darling. Wait until you are at a higher point. Next, go to the restaurant that is a mixture of fire and water."

This was another fairly obvious place—a floating restaurant that had burned to the water some years ago. He went there and received another note containing a clue. This sent him to another spot, then another, and so on throughout the evening. Finally, he received the order to go to "The restaurant in the building that is not

the tallest, and surely not the most Fair, but does belong
in Space." He was tired of these clues but was grateful
that this was likely the denouement—the meeting itself—at a city landmark.

He arrived at the Space Needle and asked for a table,
saying he was expecting a companion. He left his nickname from the ad—Hamlet—with the hostess. He sat
among the Japanese tourists and families from the suburbs, waiting for a final clue or for the appearance of the
woman he was sure he loved. He was hoping that this
time he would receive more than a clue—that she would
walk directly up to the table and they would begin their
relationship drinking and dining at the top of the city.
It was a touristy fantasy, but he was romantic enough to
appreciate such an ending.

He sat for more than an hour before a beautiful
woman approached his table. She was about thirty and
dressed in black. Her features were refined, her hair per-
fectly coifed, her complexion flawless. As she neared
him she smiled and handed him an envelope.

He took the envelope but ignored it and looked at
her. "Are you . . . ?" he asked.

"Am I . . . what?" she responded.

"I'm waiting for someone," he said.

"I'm sorry, sir, I check hats and coats—someone
gave me a note to be delivered to your table."

"Did you see them?"

"My manager gave it to me."

"Oh."

She left and he opened the envelope.

The note read, "You are at the tallest point, but at your lowest point. You have found me, yet you will not find me. You know me, yet you do not know me. You must do me a favor now, my darling, a favor I have waited for all this evening. Go outside. Climb to the edge. Jump.

"Consider it a down payment."

Simon couldn't figure out the clue.

Down payment? What did it mean? Of course it didn't mean he should jump—but that's what it said. Simon read the note over and over, but he couldn't figure it out. Would she provide more clues?

A waitress walked toward him with a drink and placed it on his table.

"This is for you," she said.

"Who ordered it?"

"I'm not sure—the bartender gave it to me."

Simon looked around seeking clarification. Perhaps his intended was at another table. He didn't see anyone who looked a likely candidate.

He wasn't sure if she would come here, or if he was to go somewhere else. He tasted the drink. It was sweet—Kahlua, he thought, combined with something else—possibly vodka. It had a name, but he couldn't remember it—he seldom ordered such common drinks, preferring European liqueurs such as Chartreuse and

Cointreau.

He drank it—it was free. He waited.

He sat at his table, drinking, and reading the note and waiting for more clues.

Days later he was still clueless.

COMMON CAUSES OF OMNIPOTENCE

Murphy's psychiatrist picked up the little clock from his desk and shook it. He had been complaining during the past two visits that it wasn't running right—too slow or something.

"Damn thing," he said, shock testing it against the desk with a force of several Gs. "Now what was it you were whining about this week?—something about your sex life?"

"Yes," Murphy replied timidly. "I'm a little early."

"Early?" The psychiatrist turned the clock around and looked at it. "You mean this little bastard is running fast as well? Go back out into the waiting room then."

"No—I mean early in bed . . . you know."

"I've been wanting to mention," the psychiatrist said, sounding irritated, "that I've been counting the number of times you say 'you know,' and I've come up with an average figure of 200 times per hour—a fifty-minute hour I might add. Did you realize that?"

"No."

"So you're *early*," he said, his eyes narrowing. "*How* early?"

"About a day."

"A day? You mean you . . . a day early?"

"Uh huh. As a result I'm making a lot more dates, but not enjoying them. I never show up."

"How are you meeting all these women?"

"Oh, different ways. I just talk to them . . . whatever . . . I just try to date the women I meet, that's all."

"And it works?"

"Sure. Except for the fact that I never go out with them. They say yes."

"So a lot of them say yes, huh?"

"Yeah, sure."

"Why?"

"I guess maybe they sense that I'm kind of innocent, at least right now. And I'm also relaxed, but at the same time very interested in them. I guess they take it as a compliment rather than feeling threatened. I mean, after all . . ."

". . . you'll never show up."

"Right."

"How did this start? And how can you stand it? You've got all these women available, but you never get to them. You must have done something to get it started."

"Well, it was a few months ago. I was really dis-gusted with dating women I didn't like. I did it just so I could go to bed with them. I felt too driven, you know, at their mercy. I woke up nearly every morning feeling a sense of self-loathing."

"Intuitive feelings can be very accurate."

"I was desperate to change my life. I couldn't stand that, you know, waiting until after the first time I went to bed with a woman to realize whether I liked her or not. I mean, right afterward I could think again, and lots of times when I came to I was with someone I really didn't like very much. It was very disturbing."

"You didn't like *any* of them?"

"I don't think so—I never gave any of them my right name."

"What is it you hate about women?"

"I don't hate women. I like them quite a lot. They're usually very nice to me. They're often kind and likeable. Some of them have very soft skin, too. I miss that."

"Then what's wrong with them?"

"I just don't have much in common with most of them. They have Tupperware parties. They shop at

Sears for lawn furniture. They expect me to send them roses."

"What's wrong with that?"

"I was raised not to be romantic or sentimental. I can't get excited by someone whose idea of luxury is Home Box Office."

"So you decided to do without women?"

"No. I decided I would find a way to go out only with women I really liked. What I hated was that I would go out with these women I didn't like just because I was really horny."

"So how did you find out if you really liked them?"

"Well, every time I thought about calling someone I'd masturbate first."

"So did that work?"

"Sort of. I stopped going out completely. Every time I masturbated I lost interest in making phone calls."

"I see the problem."

"After awhile I tried to stop it and start calling them again, but now I can't resist—sometime before I go to pick them up I masturbate. As a result . . . ."

"I *do* have a suggestion."

"What?"

"Become celibate."

"That's about what I'm doing now—in a way."

"No no. Not quite. I mean in the future when you go to pick up your date, go out no matter what happens beforehand. Don't even think about going to bed. Get to know your date as a person. Like her, or don't like her, for herself—not because she's sexy. See what happens. Sooner or later things will return to normal, then you can have a good relationship that also includes sex."

"I'm sorry, Doc, but I've already tried that."

"Really?"

"It was the first thing I tried. I mean, it's obvious. I dated one woman for months and slept with her without making love. I liked the affection and we developed quite a good rapport."

"And your sex life didn't return to normal?"

"No. The more celibate I was the more I liked it. I even became more omnipotent."

"You mean impotent."

"No, omnipotent. I no longer felt I had base human needs like sex. I was above that. I didn't have to depend on women or go to bed with women I didn't like, and this gave me a feeling of power. I used to wake my woman friend in the middle of the night and tell her about these feelings. Often at night I felt so wise and powerful I thought I could go outside and create a tree. 'Only God can make a tree,' she told me, but I figured, what the hell, I would try anyway."

"I don't have to ask how that went."

"Well, I don't know. It was kind of interesting actually. I mean, of course I didn't create a tree, but I did have a nice relationship with them. When I was a kid I spent most of my time climbing them. And when I was

going through puberty, one of the first times I ever masturbated was in a tree. I mean, in a manner of speaking,
God wasn't the only one who ever made a tree."

"That's disgusting."

"That's what she said. We stopped dating. I tried to
go back to other women and a normal life. Now I'm
kind of stuck."

"You don't have any ideas?"

"Well, I have been running a personals ad."

"How would that help?"

"I'm looking for a woman who grew up as a
tomboy—someone who likes to climb trees . . . ."

ALPHABETICAL ARDOR

Brian Down sat in a wooden chair behind the counter of the book store reading *Finnegans Wake*. He wasn't reading it so much as he was abstracting it. He was counting the punctuation. He was such a failure in a literary sense that even this not-entirely pointless activity was derivative—he had read about it in a novel by Richard Brautigan. As he proceeded with his count he duly entered the findings into a calculator. This activity gave him the appearance of erudition and quiet efficiency to suit his position as bookseller.

The shop that employed him for six dollars an

hour from nine to five, eleven to six on Saturdays, was a small hole-in-the-wall repository of culture situated equidistant from a university, a suburban shopping center, and a colossal laundromat—a coincidence of geography that affected its personality. It was a masterwork of the eclectic. New Directions paperbacks commingled with books like *Advice from Stars of Soap Opera*. Literary quarterlies shared living space with *Reader's Digest* and *Mademoiselle*. On the counter in front of Brian, Jean-Paul Sartre stared myopically from the book jacket of a critical anthology toward the lurid cover of a Harlequin Romance. Nearby, Erica Jong and Danielle Steele, covers touching, resented integration—especially Erica.

The clientele was also predictably mixed. Readers of *Penthouse*, smelling of leather and Coors, jostled gentle married ladies thumbing through *Soap Opera Digest*, confirming their notions of life outside the home as a dangerous and hostile experience. Ascetic young men wearing wire-rimmed glasses demurred to aloof females scouring the shelf of books marked *WOMYN*.

These circumstances caused Brian, in the prime of his hormonal, if not intellectual life, to spend most evenings counting the punctuation in *Finnegans Wake*.

Brian, a small dark-haired man of thirty, shy and cerebral, had sought employment as a bookseller, hoping to activate a social life that had undergone cryogenic immersion. Earlier in his life he had formed friendships easily, without regard for common tastes or interests, much as an indifferent shopper would buy generic beer. Now he sought only those who shared his intellectual obsession. The position at the counter of a bookstore had always seemed pivotal, central to the action that took place there, much as a teacher provided leadership to a classroom, or as a director demanded the attention of his actors. Brian had often approached such counters seeking direction and advice, and, if the clerk was female, occasionally tried to strike up a conversation.

However, having succeeded in finding such employment himself, Brian had discovered that most of his customers were remarkably self-sufficient, treating him as a mere adjunct to the cash register. If he made a gesture of friendship toward a customer, a witty remark about a selection, for instance, he usually received the type of welcome accorded Satan worshipers by evangelists.

He had resorted, therefore, to feigned indifference toward his customers, an attitude just shy of disdain. He intended to punish them with the loss of his scintillating and witty company.

When Brian closed the shop at five, he tallied the day's sales, after removing his punctuational sums from the calculator and marking them into the appropriate pages of Joyce's novel. Then he deposited the day's receipts at the bank. From there he proceeded to his apartment on his bicycle, a Gitane that had cost him five hundred dollars of his meager salary. He had hoped it would impress some young woman, but so far he had met no young women to impress. The closest he had come were the two teenaged girls in a Subaru who had nearly run him over one night as he pedaled home. At his apartment he prepared a supper of Knorr oxtail soup, French bread, and unfiltered apple cider. He sat for awhile with his phone, looking through an address book, trying to find someone to call. There were numbers in the book, but most of them dated from the time he had attended the self-same university that now provided many of his customers. Most of his old friends were now husbands and wives—corporate lawyers or budding entrepreneurs. One of his old buddies did come into the shop frequently, to pick up copies of *Fortune* and *Self,* but never acknowledged their former kinship. His old gang had gradually resigned from his life and no one new had signed up. He had become more and more preoccupied with absorbing everything literate, and became more isolated. Finally, he had even given up on literacy and had moved on to the more abstruse objective of compiling data on the punctuation in various literary icons. He had a notion, loosely forming, that he would connect this information in some fashion as the basis of a master's thesis. (Though he had not yet applied, having heard a rumor that the department this year did not favor projects that would require committee members to bring scratch paper to the oral exam.) He had also considered trying to take one of the more respected works, the *Alexandria Quartet* perhaps, and break it down into its component parts—counting each "the," "an," "ennui," and "schemata." He would list the parts on a huge chart (it would require a new apartment), and reuse every word, colon, and ellipsis in a new work, ideally the opposite in theme and structure. He had tried this a couple of times with fillers from the *Reader's Digest* and had been pleased to have the resulting pieces accepted by *Schizoid,* a quarterly well respected among nihilists, which had a wide circulation due to its placement in the waiting rooms of many mental health centers.

Brian eventually gave up staring at his address book, an alphabetical cemetery of friendship, returned the phone to its customary place, and dug his portable tele-vision from beneath a cardboard box marked *Paris Review.* He positioned it on the floor and tuned it to a rerun of *Leave It To Beaver.*

Half an hour with Hugh Beaumont and Barbara Billingsly soothed his nerves, after which he stared at the television screen without connecting the images to theme or story until a couple of hours later when his attention returned during a commercial for a popular panty liner. This prompted him to shave, shower, and ride his bike to Goodies, a local tavern with a Foosball table and a rock band. There he stood around drinking light beer, being bruised by the elbows of men larger and more assertive than himself, while a female singer

performed a series of gyrations that confirmed the continued existence of his libido.

As usual on this type of outing, the evening ended
with Brian leaving, half-sotted and morose, before the
bar closed. Outside, next to the spot where his bicycle
was tethered, he found a young woman sitting on the
curb. She was moaning and holding her head.

Brian wasn't very good at initial meetings, but managed to ask her if she needed an ambulance or anything.

"No," she responded, "Do you need a shrink or anything?"

Brian answered that he didn't, that he was just fine
on any of five or six types of major tranquilizers.

Their verbal dueling continued for several minutes,
during which time Brian found his point had become
quite dull. Still, they agreed to have coffee—as she was
moaning because of an overdose of wine flips and
thought caffeine might help.

As they talked, Brian's daydreams focused on a
small house in the suburbs with a den, and a lawn-
mower in the garage. The girl was young and impres-
sionable, but a good listener, evidenced by Brian's two-
hour monologue. When they finally got around to talking about her, when he asked her what she "did," she
said something startling.

"I'm a file clerk," she told him. "I alphabetize
things."

"You . . . what?"

"Alphabetize things. You know: a, b, c . . . ."

"Of course!" exclaimed Brian, as though he had just this moment grasped the Congressional budget process. "That's the answer! That's how I'll do it! I'm sorry, but I have to leave." And without further concern for their budding relationship, Brian left, not even bothering to add the girl's name and number to his address book. He returned home, broke out several hundred three-by-five index cards, and started to work.

Six months later the results of his labor seemed more commercial than academic, so he took the project to a publisher, and within weeks had a decision and a healthy advance for his magnum opus. The book: *Finnegans Wake: In Dictionary Form (with annotations)*, was a huge seller in the tradition of *The Book of Lists* and made Brian comparatively wealthy. Authors besieged him with requests that their books be honored with similar treatment.

Still, no one would talk to Brian, or be his companion—not even his publisher. After awhile he consoled himself by acquiring a cat that he paper-trained on twenty-five percent rag-content bond.

SILENT WOMEN

During the first winter after his divorce, Milo became engaged to a silent woman. He dated her for the
usual male reasons—she was a favorable cross between
Sharon Stone and the Virgin Mary. When he first asked
her out he probably wouldn't have cared if she had admitted to being a variety of marsupial, much less worry
about her conversational skills. She was pretty and he
was tired of talk. He had been raised, after all, during
the era of Donna Reed, Loretta Young, and Florence
Henderson, none of whom blabbed a lot, but if they
did, said little of consequence.

He retained his own political and philosophical fervor, and Janie's responses seemed just about right. She would nod, and from time to time, when he said something really profound, rub his thigh. At the time this was what he considered a supportive relationship.

After awhile though, quite inexplicably, he became bored with this and tried to get her to talk. Agreement, after all, was no good unless it was detailed and indicated at least a third grade understanding of the subject—which was certainly his understanding in most cases.

He began encouraging her to speak out more often, to give her opinion, to make the occasional quip, to add to the conversation, to *TALK* for Pete's sake.

To which she finally responded by speaking as they were seated for dinner, waiting for the return of the Maitre'd—Mabel. Milo had been encouraging Janie to speak up, to give her witty opinion on the upcoming elections, to tell him what she thought of the movie they had just seen—a matinee (special rates you know). He had been encouraging her this way for about half an hour, just letting her know her opinion was valued.

Suddenly she said, "I'll speak up when I feel like it. Who do you think you are? Always bugging me about talking. I can't help it that I'm not a blabbermouth like you."

"Give it to him, honey," said Mabel, who had recently returned with the Special, graciously served on two Navy plates. Mabel looked like a refugee from Abbott and Costello movies, and Milo was hoping she would soon be deported back into them.

After her comment, Janie sat silently the rest of the meal. It was a mute point, but a good one.

Afterward, it was even more difficult to get a verbal response from her. True, from time to time, watching a talk show late at night, she would chortle or snigger, but that was the extent of her expression. She wouldn't even roll her eyes in disbelief if she didn't like something. She would just turn up missing shortly after the show started.

In many other ways she was still perfect for the relationship he wanted—she was a striking woman who made him look good wherever they went.

He thought he could tolerate her taciturn behavior, but eventually he reacted to her silence, perhaps even over-reacted, and gave way to an urge to make things difficult for her.

They were to attend a lecture at the university. When they arrived on stage through a back door, Janie realized he had arranged for her to be a featured speaker. And she *did* speak on that occasion—she excommunicated him in both Roman and Anglo-Saxon slang before ending their speaking engagement.

Even he couldn't quite understand his cruelty on that occasion, and promised it would never happen again. He told her he had become so frustrated by her silence that he had lost emotional control. After a time she forgave him, though she seldom spoke again.

Things went smoothly, if silently for a time, but again her silence began to drive him mad. Rather than express his own emotions verbally, he allowed them to fester and accrue. He resisted his urges for a time, but eventually, in his madness, he made more cruel and unusual arrangements.

The arrangements involved a quiet dinner together at his friend's restaurant. It was on a Tuesday evening that they were seated at a quiet table, the only one on a platform above the main floor of his friend's small bistro.

Milo excused himself to go to the bathroom. While he was gone, show lights came on, putting Janie under the spotlight. The platform was a small stage and Tuesday was open-mike night. An emcee walked onto the stage, handed her the microphone and announced that she would be singing a version of "My Way."

After that their relationship could have been described as "strained," though "nonexistent" would also have been accurate. He had not stayed at the restaurant after her performance had been announced and therefore had not seen the consequences. He was cruel enough to arrange the show, but too squeamish to watch.

He saw her only one more time—when she was back in town on a nightclub tour. The club appearance he had arranged had been more successful for her than he might have expected. Janie, facing the crowd, was finally angry and for the first time in her life began to talk. And she talked about Milo. And she was funny. The more cruelly she described his behavior, the more the audience laughed. A show-business agent among the crowd took an interest in her and tutored her. He arranged a tour in which she simply described her relationship with Milo. Later, she moved to Los Angeles and became a sit-down comic, continuing her vicious monologue about men who talked too much.

Milo not only missed her company but felt that he deserved at least some credit for having ended her silence, and once tried to see her during a local appearance. He left his name with her manager, but instead of seeing Janie he was visited by King Kong's little brother who insisted he tour the bottom of the dumpster in the alley.

Milo avoided women altogether for a while but then met Maria, a dark haired woman who had features and elastic skin that caused his glands to sing the major arias from *The Ring of the Nibelungs*. After about a week with Maria, he had regained ten to fifteen percent of his IQ, and he tried to figure out what it was he liked about her.

She was attractive—that was most of it—and her silence tended to indicate approval. How could he go wrong spending time with a good-looking woman who

found in him no fault and indulged his wish to be mas-
saged with the olive oil from jars of artichoke hearts?
These relationships with silent women always seemed so
auspicious in the beginning. After all, there was the at-
traction of always having an appreciative audience, one
which is constantly giving a silent ovation of approving
nods and smiles. Unlike many women, the silent ones
didn't demand to know his IQ and income, but instead
smiled a lot and kneaded the muscles of his thighs.

The difficulty, however, was what he had just experienced with Janie. When the ongoing silence begins to
irritate, there is no end to it, no relief in sight, for it is
impossible to learn from a silent woman the reasons for
her silence.

Though he did *try* to learn this from Maria.

"Why won't you talk to me?" he asked one night in
the throes of post-coital depression. "I need a response.
I need feedback." Maria kissed his cheek and shrugged.
"Can't you say something?" he asked, becoming more
irritated.

Maria struggled for words. She took several deep
breaths. She rolled her eyes upward. "Well," she said,
and evidently exhausted by the effort, fainted.

When she came to, he said, "You've got to say *something*. You've *got* to. I can't stand this anymore. I'm
going quietly mad. I don't want to do to you what I did
to my last girlfriend. You've got to help me understand
or I'll have to leave."

Maria got out of bed, leaving him to think she was suggesting he take his threatened course, but returned a few minutes later carrying a five-by-eight manila card. It turned out to be a report card from her grade school. It had her name on it and the name of the school, and a list of classes with grades, all of which were quite good. At the bottom of the card under a row of lines with the heading ˝class participation˝ he saw the comment written by the teacher. ˝Who?˝ it read.

Somehow, somewhere along the way, Maria had disappeared from the audible world. She was still visible in the flesh and in writing, but even this was kept to the minimums demanded by course requirements. She seemed completely afraid that her uncensored thoughts should escape and be subject to public scrutiny, and she had therefore kept them secret. She couldn't say anything wrong if she said nothing at all.

He talked to her about this over the next few months and encouraged her to start therapy, to begin building confidence. She responded more positively than Janie and soon they were having three- or four-minute conversations daily. He looked forward to this brief intercourse, though it was shorter than the other kind. Considering the other comforts of the relationship, he began to have great hopes for their future.

But Maria had been in therapy no more than two months when she returned from her group one night and announced she had something important to say to him. He sat beside her on the couch, listening carefully for her words—they were so sparse that he savored each one.

"I've been trying to say this for months," she told him, with some effort, "but it's been very hard because as you know it's not easy for me to express my feelings."

"I know, Maria, but I've been some help with that, haven't I?"

"Yes, you have. Enough so I can say what I'm going to say now."

"Yes, dear, what's that?"

"Milo, I'd like you to get out of here."

"Gee, you've finally developed a sense of humor. That's pretty funny," he said, but the humor of the moment had dissipated somewhat, as she had by this time locked him into a half-Nelson and was moving him toward the front door like a freight-train crossing Iowa.

And that was the last he heard from Maria.

After that he decided it was better to allow silent women their silence rather than to encourage them to talk.

"You don't say much," he told his date one night some months after his eviction by Maria. His date bathed in the glow of a candle and he was lit by a German white wine.

"I've always been quiet," she said, "but I've always wanted to do something about it—learn to talk more.

Maybe someone who is more talkative could do something to help me. What do you think?"

He leaned toward her.

"Shut up and kiss me," he said.

He hoped she would think he was just being romantic.

TIN MAN
(A cautionary tale for intelligent machines)

Seymour was a tin man. Not tin exactly but a molybdenum alloy close enough in appearance to tin that no one but an engineer or a fussbudget would notice the difference.

Seymour was mechanical and electronic. Some called him electro-mechanical but not when any software engineers were nearby.

He had circuits that allowed him to walk and talk and think thoughts that were slowed only when several circuits tried simultaneously to access his CPU. (This was the cybernetic equivalent of walking and chewing gum at the same time.) He appeared more thoughtful and a little slower than many of his fellow products, who were developed later, after the chief engineer took the Cure. Seymour was, however, the same as the others in some respects—he wore the same green plaid jacket similar to one that had for years been the engineer's favorite. And he had the same face stamped from sheet metal and resembling nothing so much as a Jell-O mold.

Seymour lived with others of his kind in an inner-city housing project, a cybernetic ghetto. Only units with optical crystal memory who had more flexible intelligence and were noted for their wit at parties were allowed to live near the human communities. The highest aspiration the lower order units could hope for was the occasional opening in situation comedy.

During the day Seymour worked at McDonalds as a fry cook. He didn't mind the work (he was programmed not to mind it), and it paid his electric bills, although it was seldom enough to provide any but the most modest of updates, modifications, and maintenance recommended by his manufacturer. He lived a quiet, seldom stimulating life.

He most enjoyed real-time meetings with a cybernetic cosmetician named Molly. Their dates were arranged by a mainframe computer. These giant computers, in decline for many years, had come back into vogue in order to control the many smaller computers, including the digital souls of the cybernetics. The big computers were quite effective, their one downside being the tendency of their electronic voices to emulate a German accent.

Dates with Molly were quite pleasant, although gender was less significant than in the human community. This was partly due to sexual functioning having been designed by an engineer who lacked sufficient knowledge. It was a seldom discussed cultural phenomenon common among software engineers.

Other pleasures in his existence included learning numbering systems, listening to computer tapes, and shocking small web-footed creatures at the park.

When Seymour was twenty years old he was retired from McDonalds and presented with a going-away gift. The gift was an "expansion" module that was said to require only a few milliamps. When plugged in it would allow the cybernetic the particularly human experience called "inductive leap." This rise in consciousness was described to him as being analogous to a thought process outlined by Albert Einstein in letters to Ernst Mach. It portended a remarkable intellectual experience.

After the rituals of departure were satisfied, Seymour rushed to his cubicle and plugged in the unit, only to discover he had been misled. The module, he learned later, had been based on the life and works of Samuel Beckett, who espoused a view that all existence is essentially lonely and pointless. Seymour wrote three one-act plays before the program ended. These were later produced as cabaret entertainment for an increasing population of optical crystal cybernetics who had been adversely affected by laser radiation. Seymour afterward never used the module, but loaned it out to friends he considered overly optimistic.

Retirement was uneventful. Seymour's pension was small and he seldom had dates with Molly. Such meetings were now unlikely as she had managed several updates denied him and preferred the company of the ubiquitous younger generation.

When Seymour was twenty-seven, his manufacturer went out of business and he was forced to rely upon cheap commercial houses for his spare parts. He began feeling poorly, thought less clearly, and frequently found himself waiting at the wrong bus stop. Late in his thirtieth year, one of his power supplies failed. His protection circuits switched him over to the spare supply, but not before his motor circuits and memory (short-term was volatile) were affected. He had lost much of his joy and optimism, which in any case had been only slightly superior to that of a well-maintained toaster. The men at the repair shop told him spare parts were impossible to get, as the industry was standardizing on a new Japanese model. If he had the money, they could of course rebuild him, but they weren't sure his original memories could be retained—at least not as ˮhis.ˮ

ˮIf there are two boats,ˮ said the technician, ˮand all the parts from the first boat are used to replace the parts in the second boat, is the new boat the first boat or the second boat? And where did the other boat *go* anyway?"

This riddle itself did some software damage to Seymour, but he got the gist.

"Of course, if you want, we could scrap you out," said the technician.

Seymour thought awhile, then, seeing no alternative, said, "Scrap me out, but please notify my friend." And he gave them Molly's address. His programmed politeness was strong enough that he wanted to spare her the inconvenience, in the unlikely event she wanted another meeting with him, of finding him unaccountably unavailable.

Other than the brief arc when the technician cut the power, it didn't hurt, and his memories faded peacefully and slowly enough that he could savor them.

EAST MEETS WEST; TWAIN STILL ABSENT

On a recent weekend, I stood in the checkout line of the local Safeway, so wired on caffeine that I was arcing to the produce scale. I held, nestled in my transfixed arms, three different kinds of coffee, copies of *The New Yorker*, *Vanity Fair*, *New Man*, *New Woman*, *Esquire*, *The New York Times*, a carton of Camel Lights (I don't smoke—my cat does), and a five-pound bag of coffee nips. I had been up for about twenty-four hours on an assignment and I figured it would be late Sunday night before I would have it ready.

As I waited for the checker to process the purchases

of a housewife ahead of me, a frizzy-haired young woman behind me in the line looked up through her bottle-thick glasses and said, "You from New Yawk, or L.A.?"

"I'm from here," I said, meaning the Northwest.

"You kiddin'? Here? I meant *originally.*"

"I'm from *here* originally," I told her. "What about you?"

"You kiddin'? New Yawk. I thought you was from New Yawk, too. You just look like you oughta be a New Yawkuh—what with all that coffee and all."

"Nah, I'm just the bean buyer for Hills Brothers," I said, dropping my packages in my mirth.

"Yeah, I know what ya mean," she replied. "That's very funny." She kicked one of my bags of coffee toward me as I struggled to pick things up. "I guess you ain't a New Yawkuh."

Then she squeezed ahead of me in the line.

I gathered myself up and followed her to the checker. She paid, grabbed her bag, looked at me with unconcealed scorn and said, "I don't know how I coulda thought you was from New Yawk."

"I was never fooled," I told her, but by this time she had left.

"Wow, buddy," said the checker, a comely blond in Birkenstocks and a blue smock. "I think your aura shrunk."

I set my purchases on the counter and she rang

them up with authority, talking as she keyed the register.

"Yeah, those New Yorkers—they can zing you. You ain't the type to get along with them—you're too laid back, you know. I mean, like, you remind me more of this guy I used to go with back in Del Mar. I mean, he was laid back.

"So is this going to be cash or check?" she asked, dropping my receipt on the counter.

When I got home I noticed that a certain Jell-O-like feeling remained from the encounter with the Empire State expatriate. I tried eating Lorna Doones, then Sugar Smacks, but that didn't seem to help so I went out shopping for socks at the mall. I've always found buying socks soothing, especially if they let you try them on.

Afterward, though, I still felt a niggling insecurity, a sense of failure as a man for this shortage of aggression—it wasn't a new insecurity, one of my platoon sergeants had noticed it as well. So I gave my friend Ned a call in the hope he could shore up my flagging self-image.

We met for a drink at an intellectual pick-up bar about midway between our domiciles. I sat listening to the music and drinking a Zombie as I waited for Ned. I usually got quite a bit of action in places like this because they played rock music and the only parts of my body I could ever get to keep time with music were my eyes, a habit which was subject to varying interpretations, but which usually resulted in my being slapped

several times before I could have been described as being even slightly tight. The third woman had just left my
table after having dumped my drink in my lap and calling me "frosh," (we were very near a university) when
Ned arrived.

"You're really going through them," he said, notic-
ing my newly emptied drink.

"Yeah. Boy, they're sure cold."

Ned rolled his eyes, which I thought rather
dangerous, and ordered a Tanqueray and tonic. I had
met Ned at a writing conference and we had become fast
friends, although we had slowed quite a bit since. He
was a writer of ghosted autobiography, a field for which
he was well suited as he had several autonomous
personalities.

I told him the story of the New Yorker in the grocery
store. "Boy, they sure are assholes," I said, summing up
the experience.

Ned impaled me on the end of a hairy finger with a
speed and panache that made me think he had been
watching a lot of fencing movies. "I don't suppose you
know where I was born, do you?"

"Connecticut?" I replied, wondering if this was a
trick question.

"I was *raised* in Connecticut," he responded, "but I
was born in New York."

"I see." I had a feeling I wasn't going to get a lot of
support from Ned.

"Bring me another T & T," Ned told a passing waitress, "and bring this woodsy Northwest creature a Pine-
Sol."

When Ned left I had to think about the implications
of his and the New Yorker's comments. I mean, were
Northwesterners really more naive and unsophisticated
than people from other areas? It was a question I was
still considering a few days later at a box social at the
church. I and Trina, the woman whose lunch I had
chosen, were hitting it off pretty well, mostly due to the
fact that the blouse she had chosen to wear didn't keep
her breasts confined so much as on probation.

"Have you ever gotten into Eastern philosophy?" she
asked as I was nibbling a chicken thigh.

"Not really," I replied. "I don't like the way they
think in New York and New Jersey."

"Cute," she said, "you must be from here."

I *felt* my aura shrinking this time.

"You from New York?" I asked nervously.

"No—I can't stand New Yorkers. I'm from L.A. But
I still don't like precious humor as much as you Northwesterners. I mean Richard Brautigan was enough, but
after all he was from *Northern* California. In L.A. we
like a little more of an edge. You ever read Bukowski?"

"No. Is he good?"

"He's good—*and* he's dead, too. He was an asshole,
actually. I was just using him as an example of 'edge.' "

I had sort of lost my taste for chicken, but a piece of

it continued to hang from my mouth anyway. I asked,
"Well . . . what are you doing at a church social then?"

"Only way I could figure to get laid," she said, "The
men in this town are so *backward*."

I don't know exactly how it happened, her technique was so smooth, but somehow I ended up being
persuaded to return to her apartment to take a look at a
screenplay she had written before leaving L.A. (She had
been writing about wild mushrooms since moving to the
Northwest.)

I never did see the screenplay and ended up, before
the afternoon was even middle-aged, performing gyrations somewhere between bumper cars and the tilt-a-
whirl. During all this activity she found time to tell me
her life story (it had already been filmed about someone
else), the plot of her screenplay, plus complain about the
local job market.

"They don't even *do* here what I did for a living in
L.A. I mean this place is that *small*.

"Then there are the men—what twerps. I mean it's
the first time I ever missed Cole."

"Who's Cole?"

"My ex old-man. That's not his real name, it's a
nickname. He had to change his real name after this soft
drink company found out about it. His real name is
their registered trademark and they've had the rights to
it since 1890 or something." She sat up in the waterbed,
causing me to capsize.

I righted myself and asked, "What does Cole do?"

She spat her Juicy Fruit gum across the room. It thwacked the inside of a tin wastebasket.

"Well, a couple of years ago he went into one of these places that test for aptitude, you know?"

"Yeah?"

"I never got the results of the test, but I gather from his behavior that he was best suited to be a heroin addict."

"Oh."

"It's just as well. He never had the class for cocaine and he would have run into more trademark problems anyway."

Trina pushed up against me, bringing her face next to mine. Her tongue emerged and licked forcefully against my lips. I pulled away.

"What's wrong?"

"I just didn't like that."

"You pulled away like you loathed it."

"I didn't loathe it."

"You did. Admit it."

"I didn't loathe it."

"You loathed it, admit it."

"Well . . . just a little."

"Get out of here, creep!"

When I got home I called another friend—Leon. We went out for coffee. Leon doesn't drink or smoke or ride in American cars, so our activities are limited. A conversation with Leon is sort of a progress report in the style of recent graduates of personal transformation seminars.

"I'm really cranking," said Leon of his work, which was not mechanical at all. "I'm finally getting clear that this is what I want to do. More important, my boss is getting clear that this is really what he wants to pay me for.

"And Marla is great," he said, shaking his head in amazement that Marla was great, sort of disgusted-like at how marvelous she was. "We were at a party last night and she said she, you know, wanted to 'go for it' with me. I told her, 'Yeah, I'm ready to go for it with you, too, just as long as you let go of these old trips, just as soon as you get clear.'

"It's kind of a situation really, because Caryl also told me she wanted to 'go for it' with me. But I don't know about Caryl. She's from New York and they have a lot of aggression and competitiveness." He grimaced disapproval. "I don't think I could ever really get clear with her. It's, like, very unlikely, dig?" He looked at me genuinely questioning did I dig.

"I think I know what you mean," I replied.

"I mean like the time she told you to get out of her house because you didn't want to listen to the Erica Jong album . . . ?"

"That was a long time ago."

"And what about when she was teaching her daughter about sex and we were at a party and Myra pointed at you and said, 'What about him, mommy? Does he have a penis, too?' "

"I don't want to talk about this, Leon."

"So Caryl said, 'No, honey, not him—probably not.'"

"I'd rather not talk about that, Leon."

"It was probably embarrassing, but after all if it's not true, it's not a problem. We all have to deal with the truth."

"You want to know the truth, Leon?"

"I've already read all of Ram Dass."

"I mean the truth right now, Leon."

"What's the truth right now?"

"I'm really glad I already *know* you're from out of state."

SHORT WOMEN

The light in the singles bar was dim. Ponsett could barely see the cutie-pie in the halter top and Calvin Kleins, moving like a cocktail shaker to the Reggae beat. She was about four feet eleven inches, a size which, when issued in the feminine gender, caused huge hormonal rushes in Ponsett, though he was nearing middle age.

Ponsett was tall, lofty, towering, high, elevated, tree-like. The objects of his passion were tiny, abridged, short, petite, delicate—sometimes even dwarfish. He had spent his youth being persuaded to highjump and dribble inflated balls. He had ducked door frames and comments like, "How's the weather up there?" As an adult he pursued women who at one time or another had been asked to dress up and pose on wedding cakes, who needed little platforms to rest their feet on while they sat in chairs, who became exasperated with people who couldn't walk beside them without chuckling quietly.

As he walked across the dance floor toward his tiny princess, her current partner retired for the night, having, Ponsett supposed, tired of her company, or perhaps he needed to rise early the next morning to chop kindling. This usually happened when Ponsett showed interest in someone—the field was suddenly wide open.

They danced and Ponsett tried to figure out some way of getting her back to his apartment. (Carrying her seemed too obvious.) As he struggled with this dilemma he was also reviewing the doubts he always had about his obsession with short women, often the most impractical of partners for a man of his standing. He still winced as he remembered the time at *LeChic* when the waiter had brought his date a booster chair.

Ponsett had very specific height requirements for the women he admired. They could be no taller than five feet. To gauge this he had developed a fine measuring eye that even adjusted for certain height-altering accoutrements and hair styles. Once, when he mentioned to a friend that he was pining for a tiny woman of their acquaintance, his friend pointed out she wasn't all that short, that she was at least five-five.

Ponsett replied angrily that she wore platform shoes, that she always wore them and that this led to the misapprehension she was of average height. This impression, taken by most people, steamed him up; the very thought that anyone could think her taller than her true, beautiful stature was an insult. Most men undress women with their eyes. Ponsett politely removed their shoes.

But height, of course, was only one requirement. Many women pointed out to him turned out, though correct in size, to be unqualified. "Out of proportion," "Squinty-eyed," "Do you see the way she walks?" and "Too short" are some of the comments he made in response to suggested partners.

There was also a certain vulnerability required of these wee damsels. (Even if such sexist and disparaging terms were permitted, referring to them as "broads," "dames," or "skirts" always seemed to connote too great a magnitude, though "chicks" or "kittens" might have been appropriate.) To spark the great man's interest, they were required to possess a quality of gentleness, shyness, and tranquility. It always disappointed Ponsett to discover that a woman who qualified in all other areas displayed reckless vivacity, fearlessness, or, God forbid, any apparent knowledge of biology.

Perhaps it was that Ponsett, the quintessential

giant—he was nearly seven feet tall—was repelled by his own brutal dimensions, and their implications of violence, insensitivity, and limited cognition. If he could be accepted, dearly loved, and trusted by the most vulnerable and sweetest representatives of the weaker (for they seldom seemed fairer) sex, perhaps it reflected those qualities on his own massively insecure personality.

Though, possibly, it was the thrill of contrast—a magnification of his size—he desired, the sensation of Lilliputian limbs entangled with his, of those teensy ladies exploring his anatomy as though he were one of the Greater Antilles.

It was difficult for friends to assess Ponsett's feelings on this matter because, in addition to his reluctance to discuss it, he seemed so completely assimilated into a scaled-down culture. He worked as a college professor, and socialized with no apparent special awareness of size. He seemed genuinely surprised when someone, chatting amiably with him at a party, began showing signs of vertigo, or when a casual acquaintance asked him to act as a go-between in the delivery of a physical threat. Such things insulted him mildly, though he dealt with them, largely, by ignoring them, pretending for all the world that he was ignorant of their cause. He was able to maintain this aplomb even though he had often been discriminated against due to his height. He remembered with some bitterness that as a college student hitch-hiking around the country he had been offered rides only on the beds of pickup trucks.

At one time he had married a short woman and they had lived with the necessary compromises. Their apartment had contained a mixture of objects that caused visual disorientation similar to staring at an M.C. Escher engraving. Pieces of furniture were of disquietingly different dimensions. Tiny chairs were overshadowed by gigantic ottomans and three-story recliners. In the study an enormous roll-top desk, nailed to the floor by tons of gravity, dominated one corner of the room, while a tiny French Provincial writing table by Tom Thumb of California perched timidly near a window. The dining room set included a tall artist's chair for the missus, complete with a tiny set of stairs. Teensy tea cups mingled with great coffee mugs, and little baby spoons shared slots with soup spoons the size of gravy ladles. It was a visit to the three bears' house, but mama had gotten baby's things, and baby had never been conceived.

Ponsett was not married long, and the contract ended with customary bitterness. He reported their debates to friends, who imagined his voice caroming off the walls like the reverberations of a dynamite blast in the subway, while her replies sounded like Ethyl Merman speaking through a kazoo. The arguments had to do with dimensions, not size. His wife claimed Ponsett resided outside the normal three—in the area popularized by Rod Serling. Ponsett countered feebly that his wife moved around evasively in their bed at night so he could never find her. She retorted this was simply a defensive maneuver similar to the actions of mountain climbers retreating at the first sign of avalanche.

His friends were sure that the reports they heard were mere fragments—the tip of some enormous iceberg.

Ponsett was rather morose after the failure of his marriage and seemed to be quite vindictive in the matter. Several times he had to be persuaded not to run over short women who were crossing the street in front of his car, as though he had sworn a vendetta against all those innocent Kewpie dolls. He explained to his friends that since he was newly single and out of practice, it seemed the only way he could meet them.

He tried a number of therapies to rid himself of this obsession, but though he spent many a recumbent hour on couches far too short, he lost none of his enthusiasm for female half-pints.

Even now, as his dance partner smiled at him, looking very much like a tourist visiting the Eiffel Tower, he could feel nothing but admiration for her tiny qualities. To impress her he executed a difficult Swing movement, twirling her away with such force that for a moment her pins came out from under her and she was extended at the end of his arm like a paddle ball. Her wooden-soled shoes tapped a man on the periphery of the dance floor with enough force that he decided to lie this one out while another patron began administering CPR.

The diversion gave Ponsett the opportunity to lead his partner out of the nightclub. He planned to ask her if she would like to have a nightcap at his place. They were outside near a couple of cops walking their beat when he picked her up, just so he could speak to her more directly. She began screaming that she was being kidnapped by a giant.

Ponsett had no trouble explaining his way out of the misunderstanding, the only condition put upon his immediate release being that he spend a year or two in a nearby mental institution. The college he worked for graciously allowed him a permanent leave of absence and the mortgage company agreed to look after his home for the next five or six decades.

Settling in at the hospital was no problem, as the accommodations were of the same comfortable nature as those described in the movie *The Snake Pit.* The first couple of days were uneventful, passed mildly at checkers, crazy eights, and Prescription Poker (played for medication). On the third day Ponsett was ushered into an office on the top floor of the building for an appointment with his therapist, a Mrs. Foy. The office was empty when he arrived, although the chair he now occupied was still warm from the previous occupant.

"Sorry to keep you waiting, Mr. Ponsett," said a deep, comforting voice from an anteroom, preceding only by seconds its owner, who seemed to him likely to be the holder of the Guinness world record for female height.

She was so tall she could nearly touch the ceiling, even though the building they occupied had been built during the thirties when ceilings were allowed to soar. But mere height would not have impressed him so much had it not been enhanced by the shapeliness of her slim, tanned body, her honey-blond hair, and the sensuous warmth of her manner.

"How good to meet you," she said pleasantly, reaching down to his sitting position to shake his hand. "My name is Adella. I hope you're getting adjusted."

"Everything's fine," he said, making every effort to be pleasant and establish rapport with her. His body ached with his first desire for someone other than an elfin female. Her height was such that it was beyond the ability of his intuitive scale to measure. She wasn't quite his height, but she was close.

"You know why you're here, of course," said Mrs. Foy pleasantly, "and that we're trying to help you."

"I'm sure you're trying to help me," he said, "but I did wonder why I'm here—not that I mind or anything."

"Would you like to know why you're here?" she asked, crossing the room to her desk. The movement of her hips and the sight of her legs caused a reaction in some of Ponsett's anatomy analogous to the reaction of certain foods to the addition of corn starch.

"If you don't mind telling me," he said, "I feel I'd like to cooperate with you." And vice versa.

"Well, Mr. Ponsett," she paused and bit gently and sensuously on the eraser at the end of her pencil, "you seem to have this fixation, this obsession, almost this fever for the company of short women. This was all well and good, until the incident at L'Oaf in which you expressed your interest by forcing your attentions. Perhaps this was not entirely intentional, but whatever the cause, you must certainly bring this under control. You must fully realize the implications of your size. How tall are you, anyway?"

Ponsett looked at his feet and mumbled, "Not so tall. A little taller than average."

"Does seven-feet sound about right?"

"Close," he allowed, not raising his eyes.

"Face it, Mr. Ponsett. You're tall. You've probably always been tall. You've always shopped in big and tall shops. The coach probably wanted you to play basketball. You have to be careful that you don't hurt people when you shake hands. You're like a bull in a china shop when you visit someone's home.

"You're lucky to be here—most states don't even have therapy for the tall. I understand, believe me. Tall people have peculiar problems. I can help you.

"You don't have to spend your life chasing half-pints." With those words she put her hand on his shoulder and leaned her hip against his arm. "Do you?"

Ponsett didn't begin socializing with Mrs. Foy, who was divorced, until he was released from the hospital. A month afterward they moved in together.

He was happy. He was fine. He was tall.

He loved a tall woman. Whatever had caused him to pursue the un-Sanforized half of womanhood was over.

For about a month.

After that, rather than take direct physical action, Ponsett began communicating to short female pen pals at random in several nations. He was planning a brief around-the-world tour when Adella found photographs of short women beneath his handkerchiefs.

"Do you want to get over this or not?" she asked him toward the end of a heated argument.

"Of course I do," he said, truly contrite and fatigued by the ear boxing.

"Then I have a solution. It's drastic, but it will fix this permanently." She dialed a phone number.

Ponsett was scheduled for surgery the following Monday. The site of the surgery was kept a secret from him, although he knew it was somewhere in the former Soviet Union where idle scalpels and saws were anxious to be busy, even if it meant the activity bordered on the unethical or just plain odd. Two weeks later he returned on Aeroflot at the reduced height of five foot nine. They had asked the surgeons to cut him down to six feet, but apparently there had been some problem in the conversion to local units of measurement. He returned home with Adella, now completely content with her company—in fact now completely fascinated with her size and far less interested in short women who were a little too close to his own height. It was exciting to have a commanding, capable female at his beck and call. It didn't even bother him (much) that several of his colleagues at work, who had previously feared him, beat him up in the faculty cloakroom, or that students in the classroom complained they couldn't see him at the podium. He simply buried himself in Adella's flesh at night and woke up a rested happy man of average height.

Months passed before he began to notice certain peculiarities in Adella's behavior. She was staying longer and longer at the hospital—once she was gone for an entire weekend and claimed it was a new therapy for some of the patients. Ponsett was not able to determine what it was about her behavior that made him suspicious, but there was enough doubt in his mind to convince him to research the matter. Late one evening Ponsett made the journey to the hospital, and padded around the corridors (his feet were still size 14) in search of Adella.

It was as though she had left a trail for him.

He could have opened a big and tall shop with the clothing he found on the floor in her waiting room and scattered here and there in her office.

Behind the desk he found a prone Adella administering a very intimate therapy to a towering victim of short-woman syndrome.

Adella apologized long and often, but the spell was broken. Ponsett could no longer feel secure.

She liked tall guys.

And, hell, he was a midget.

THE Y-CAR

I usually drive a Saab or an Audi or a Yugo, or some other fine car like that. Occasionally, even such fine cars as these mysteriously commit suicide, and I am forced to haunt used car lots looking for something with a life expectancy at least as good as a fruit fly's. Recently, when one of my cars gave up the ghost I borrowed a car from a friend so I could chase down a replacement. My friend's car was an old Datsun station wagon with several different colored doors and a bumper sticker that read "The Cosmic Cowboy." It was a lot like driving around in a used Kleenex box and gave added motivation to my desire to get new transportation.

I used my Sundays to look at the car lots, but with-out much success. On one of these holy-day outings, as I was kicking the tires of a Vega, just out of spite, I happened to notice a pudgy compact car toward the back of the lot which looked rather new. A sign on the windshield proclaimed: THE Y-CAR. ONE ONLY. ONE OWNER.

The salesman noticed my interest the moment I touched the lot and was soon hovering around me like an overweight hummingbird, if there were ever a balding hummingbird with a blue plaid sports jacket, maroon slacks, and white shoes. He grinned and said, "Hi—name's Al. She's a little peach, isn't she?"

"Yeah, but I need a *car*. I never heard of it before. Is it something new?"

"The latest—but they're rare out West. We're lucky to have one at all—she gets good gas mileage. She's easy to maintain, parks like a dream, and this one has hardly been driven at all—an old man brought her out from New York. She's got another nice feature as well."

"What's that?"

"She talks."

"Eh?"

"Really. She has a little computer inside and it talks through a speaker in the dash—just little tips and warn-ings, like telling you to fasten your seat belt, or letting you know your gas is low or you have an engine problem."

"Really? I've heard about things like that, but I've never seen one of them. So it talks?" I leaned in to the window and looked around. It was a sunny day and the heat brought out the new car smell. It looked just like dozens of other American and imported compacts—the colorful plastic indicators and controls, the transmission shifter on the floor between the front seats.

"Like to take a drive?"

"Why not?"

So Al got the keys and we went for a drive. He drove, being a more conservative salesman I guess, just so he could show me the controls and all the features of this "little beauty."

When he started the engine, a little speaker on the dash said, "Please fasten your seat belts." It was a pleasant-sounding voice, an imitation female voice, a little deeper than average and with just the slightest trace of some European accent, probably caused by the programming somehow.

When Al shifted into reverse, the speaker said, "Be sure you can see clearly before backing the car." Al looked around really carefully, then backed up.

This went on throughout the test drive, with the speaker warning or notifying us of a variety of road and vehicle conditions, including letting Al know at one point that he was lugging the engine. You'd have thought the car had eyes of its own the way it noticed things in traffic, too, and by the time we returned to the lot, I was impressed. It seemed easy to drive; the safety warnings were not so intrusive as to be irritating, and the price was reasonable considering the car was nearly new.

I stood looking at the engine while Al continued to rattle off the good features of the car. As he closed the hood he said, "If I give you what you think you need on your car, do you think we can deal?"

"That's not my car I'm driving," I said. "I'd probably have to give you a cash down payment." Al looked relieved. "But we could probably deal. I'd like to drive it a little though, before I could get serious."

"Oh. Just a quick spin around the block, eh?" he asked, his eyebrows raising quizzically in a way that indicated he wanted yes for an answer.

"Yeah," I said, persuaded by his brows. "Just around the block."

"Okay," he said. "I know it'll run fine." Then he added, looking toward the car, "'Cause we all know what'll happen if it doesn't." I thought that was a little odd until he added, looking at me, "Because it wouldn't sell then, right?"

"Yeah, right."

Al handed me the keys and I got in.

The car started right away, then warned me about the seat belt. When I put it into reverse it warned me again about backing up. I nodded at Al as I nudged the gas pedal and backed out of the space, then put her into a forward gear and eased off the lot.

She was a nice little car—easy to handle, quick-turning, but solid and free of vibration. Nothing untoward occurred until I was in heavy traffic about a half-mile from the lot, having figured that Al's "just around the block" could be considered a strictly figurative injunction.

As I signalled to go into the left lane, a car sped up to block me. The speaker on the dash said, "Putz!"

I looked around for some other source, because I knew it couldn't be the speaker of course, but there were no cars close enough for me to hear the driver calling me names. I figured it was probably a side effect of the cold medicine I'd been taking and continued my test drive.

"Did you ever see such a meshuggener?" a voice said, and this time there was no question it was the speaker, though the accent was a little more European than the first time. I pretended not to hear.

"You don't talk, or what?" asked the voice from the speaker.

I continued pretending not to hear, and checked my surroundings to see how far I was from Al's lot. I looked for a place to turn around and hoped this voice would go away when I got out of the car. If I took it with me I was in trouble.

"Hey, boychik, I'm speaking to you. Don't be such

a shlemiel. You don't answer and I'm going to stop and you'll have to walk."

I was wheeling the car into the parking lot of a grocery store by now, figuring on a quick U-turn, a rapid retracing of my route, and a sudden leap from the car before Al could get to me. The used Kleenex box of a Datsun looked really good right now.

Just then the car went out of gear and stopped.

I looked at the gear shift lever, but it was where it was supposed to be and the brake wasn't on. I tried another gear, but it didn't work.

"So who's it going to hurt if you show a little courtesy?" said the speaker.

"Who are you?"

"Who am I? Who would I be? What is this you're riding in—a tuna can maybe? I'm not a person? I don't deserve respect?"

"You're *not* a person," I said. I tried the door, but it was locked.

"So, we won't be picky. I'm not a *person*, but I have *feelings*. I got a little *courtesy* coming."

"Okay, I'll be polite. Can we go?"

"In a minute, in a minute. Don't be so impatient. You know your gas is a little low?"

"I hadn't noticed."

"That's what I'm here for. If you were planning on stealing me and running off to Walla Walla you should know that—get gas."

"I wasn't planning on stealing you."

"Vell, you certainly vasn't going 'just around da block.'"

"I just wanted a longer test drive."

"Longer drives is what you get arrested for."

"I'm sorry, I thought it would be okay."

"So it's okay, then. Al just didn't want me to talk to you anyway. What's he afraid of? He thinks it's such a crime I talk. He thinks I won't sell. You like me don't you?"

"Sure I do," I said, pulling on the door handle again.

"Then why are you trying to get out?"

"Can we go now? Can we just *go?*"

"Vut a nag! Of course we can go." The car jumped into gear and crept forward. I took control of the steering wheel and gave her some gas. I turned on to the road again toward the used car lot. I had traveled farther than was wise considering the situation.

Things were going normally and I thought I was out of trouble, then after a brief silence the voice in the dash said, "You're not mad at me are you?"

"Oh no, of course not."

"You shouldn't be. It's not a crime to be friendly. Al, he never lets me talk. He says he can't sell me if I talk to people, but how are you going to find out anything if you don't talk, I ask you?"

"I can't think of any way," I answered, patting my

pockets to see if I had any Valiums.

"So—what's Roseanne doing these days?" she asked. "Al never tells me about her."

"I don't know. I guess she's getting divorced."

"That was ancient history. Why don't you tell me about Pearl Harbor? I thought I would be getting news, not history. She was going to remarry someone."

"I really don't know."

"What about Liz, and Michael Jackson—what about them?"

"I'm sorry, I don't know."

"Do me a favor, boychik—don't buy me.

"Walter, Walter, Walter," she said, "*Why* did you have to go away?"

"Who's Walter?"

"The Pope. Who'd you think he would be—Walter used to own me. He died of a stroke, poor man. He used to read me the *Enquirer*. What a Shveetheart he was.

"On the other hand he was such a doormat—he would let his sister walk all over him.

"One thing—she won't do that any more—except maybe on his grave.

"Well, big spender," she said as we pulled into the car lot, "so you got back safe. Do me a favor—buy a Pinto."

We parked, and I hopped out as soon as she stopped. Al was coming out of the office.

"Decided against her, eh?"

"Well, you know . . . ."

"Yeah, I know. Jeez, what a Yenta."

"Oh, so that's what the Y stands for."

"That's right. Well, I'll find someone."

I got back into the Kleenex box and drove away.

The next weekend when I was out looking again I noticed that the Y-car was gone. I stopped in and Al told me he had sold it to a middle-aged widower.

"He loves gossip," Al said, "and he told me he doesn't mind a little nagging once in a while, or an argument now and then.

"Once in a while he has to go somewhere he doesn't want to go but, like he said, 'I was married once, so what's new?'"

THE OTHER MAN

The light in the Dew Drop Inn was the kind of illumination familiar to members of Iron Age tribes. A marimba band version of "Lady of Spain" tickled Tom's feet through the dance floor as Delores applied another suction-induced contusion to the side of his neck.

As Tom was an accountant by trade and nature, this activity was uncharacteristic. These Country-Western weekends transformed him, a la Jekyll and Hyde, into a man who not only didn't keep books, but didn't keep phone numbers or give his right name. He doubted that he would see Delores again—for that matter he couldn't

see her now. Granted, these were not mature relationships, but he considered them preferable to making
pelvic thrusts at television during *Baywatch*.

"Let's go to my car," she said, after an exploratory
lick behind his ear. Many dates like this and it wouldn't
be necessary for him to wash properly, at least not behind his ears.

"Why the car?" he asked, nuzzling her hair. He was
having difficulty thinking because of the rerouting of
blood away from his brain. "We could go to my place."

"Not tonight. My husband's here," she told him
calmly, and reached into his pocket, presumably to bor-
row a quarter.

With the mention of her husband his heart fibril-
lated a couple of times, but soon resumed operation at
ninety beats a minute. "You're married?" It was a redun-
dant, but compulsory question.

"Sort of," she said, quality-checking the inseam of
his jeans to see whether Inspector 21 had done his job.
"I don't take it too seriously."

"What about your husband? Does he take it
seriously?"

"He doesn't know what I do."

"Where is he?"

"Over there," she said, pointing to the sidelines
where a dozen drunken and displaced people sat around
at the scattered tables, drinking beer and watching the
others dance. One of the guys was bald and mid-forties,

and was drinking from a bottle of beer as he eyed them with calculated scorn. He looked like a guy who would hire himself out to kill kittens.

"That's him?" he asked, a grapefruit lodged in his throat.

"Him? Oh, no. He's over there," and she pointed to a short, red-headed guy who made Woody Allen look like a professional tackle. He wasn't even looking their way and he was soused.

Tom put his hand into Delores' rear pocket.

So he had finally seen one of these guys.

He had up to now only heard about them—the men who are, have been, or are about to be, involved with the paramour of the moment. These were the men known to the lady he shared a waterbed with in some bedroom community. They were the partners of the woman he met at a party who would tell him she was unattached when what she really meant by "unattached" was that she had been disconnected at the frontal lobes—whereas her husband was just out of town for a few days.

By having spent a long time as a single man, Tom had learned about this group of men entirely by rumor, story, and essay (when dating coeds). These were the men, for the most part, he wished not to know at all.

Tom didn't know about this group until quite late because where he came of age there was a strong social caveat against such behavior. He had wisely watched from a distance as more adventurous men sought all the married and otherwise attached women.

After his divorce, and under the influence of his seemingly uncontrollable urges, Tom more often became involved with ladies before discovering that their stability was less than gyroscopic. And he found that in some ways he preferred the company of disloyal companions. He had had enough of that circle of Hell known as a ranch-style house in the suburbs. He viewed *commitment* as a dirty word, and found that the unfaithful tended to expect less of it—not even requiring his correct name. These experiments in disloyalty led to his awareness of ˝the other man.˝

At an earlier point in life he might have assumed that the former male companions to his new women friends would naturally have been civilized human beings, good chaps with the occasional Nobel laureate thrown in. To hear the story from their former partners, however, these men represented the worst traits of Quasimodo and the Marquis de Sade.

He remembered the brief interlude some years ago with a woman he encountered at a bar and accompanied to her house—so she could give him her recipe for banana bread. She had nothing but time on her hands she said, and a willing attitude, and he assumed her to be single—if not footloose, at least not fitted for ball and chain.

They retired to her house, then to her bedroom.

Things had just gotten interesting (she had HBO) when
he heard a noise outside the house, a tapping on the
wall or window.

"What the hell was that?" he asked. They were eating
Maraschino cherries with their drinks and he had just
swallowed one, stem and all.

"It might be Max," said his acquaintance, whose
name was Shari.

"Max? Who the hell is Max?" he asked, continuing
to remain calm though his nervous system had just hit
Warp Five. "Is that your dog?"

"No. Max killed the dog."

As he was dressing he asked, "Is this person someone you know well?"

"Oh, sure," she said, "He lives here."

"Unlike the dog."

"You don't have to get upset," said Shari, extending
her lip in a pout that wasn't so convincing as her having
let the sheet drop to her waist. "I meant he used to live
here. He won't bother us. I was probably wrong. I don't
think it was Max. He's probably over it by now. We
broke up and he was bothered by it, but I think he's
over it by now. Maybe it was the neighbor's cat."

He was drawn toward Shari once more. Soon he was
back in bed. Shari had taken his head in her arms and
was being reassuring. He was, after all, quite smitten
with her and expected it to be a long-term relationship,
perhaps lasting the whole night.

Shari's affectionate attention continued as she explored areas usually reserved for nurses and dental hygienists, but her touch was much more personal.

"I'm glad you're not still involved with Max," he told her, "I'd like the chance to really get to know you."

"Well, Max and I *are* still married," she told him, without pausing in movements that were reminiscent of certain rodeo events. "So we probably shouldn't see each other too much. I mean, I think he can get ammunition after a three-day waiting period."

"Ammunition?"

"Yeah. He carries a pistol. That's how I got him to leave—I hid all his ammo."

"How long ago was this?"

"Night before last. It's okay—he won't be here until early morning—to get a few of his things. Don't worry, he promised he'd call the sheriff's office and ask one of the officers to come with him to see he didn't kill anyone."

"He promised he'd call?"

"Sure. He's violent, but he's not a liar."

She said something else, but he wasn't sure what it was because he heard it from three blocks away. He was sure the words were not compliments.

Over the years there had been others—the crazed vet with a metal plate in his head (or butter dish, he couldn't remember which) who telephoned at three a.m. to the apartment of a new woman friend. Naturally he got only one side of the conversation, but clearly overheard "grenade launcher?" and "You couldn't hit the side of a barn," during their brief discussion. Tom had hurried their telephone intercourse, and skipped the other kind so he could use the phone to call a cab.

Another girlfriend's "old man" had offered to relocate his adenoids into the jurisdiction of a proctologist. He wisely declined and applied for work in Alaska.

But now Tom had actually seen one of these people who had so threatened him over the years. It was quite reassuring that he seemed so much less frightening than Tom had imagined. He was a tiny guy and so tight that he could sit up only by grasping his beer bottle. All these years Tom's fears might have been groundless if the other men he had suspected of being terrifying killers had actually been like this guy.

But, just about the time Tom was thinking about taking Delores up on her invitation, this little shrimp stood up and walked over to them. Delores was by this time checking all his zippers to see they were operating okay. Tom suddenly felt something like the business end of a trombone in his back and thought one of the musicians was getting cute (though the presence of a trombone was a bit of a mystery). He reached to move the object and recognized it as the barrel of a .38 Special. He was familiar with it from the time as a college student in Texas when he sold guns door-to-door. Delores' hubby was wielding it, but not with so much confidence that he could be trusted to be able to tell whether or not he was killing somebody.

"Get your hands off my wife," he said.

Tom obeyed, but that still left a lot of them that was touching. Delores evidently thought the situation was under control because she was still biting the buttons off the front of his shirt.

"Well, thanks for the dance, ma'am," he said to her, trying to back away and losing quite a bit of his shirt in the process.

"You can't get out of this that easy," said her trigger-happy husband. "I saw what you were doing with her."

"That the snubnose or the police special?" Tom asked him, remembering his daddy's advice that digression is the better part of valor.

"It's the Special," said the little guy. Delores was standing between them, one hand on his shoulder and the other massaging the barrel of the pistol. Tom had the feeling she hadn't been seriously affected by the Women's Movement.

"Did you know they had a recall out on that gun?" Tom asked.

"A recall?"

"Yeah. Those things explode like crazy if you have the wrong ammunition."

"Yeah?"

"Yeah. You know how many grains are in that bullet you're using?"

The guy opened the chamber and at that moment Tom left the premises so fast you'd have thought Scotty had beamed him up.

It was an event that changed his mind about the advantages of unfaithful companions. For awhile afterward he drank at home more and tried to think of ways he could have a relationship that avoided both the problems of commitment and the dangers of infidelity. For an entire evening he considered the possibility of dating nuns. At first inspection, it seemed like such a good idea; they were committed to a male figure who was the all powerful ruler of the universe, but who was also benign and forgiving. They had given their commitment to Him and therefore had little time for the idea of marriage to a human, especially an accountant. It seemed ideal, until the 32-ounce dose of Tequila wore off, causing him to remember what most nuns looked like, that he hadn't seen them in the bars lately, and that he had an inordinate fear of wooden rulers.

SWEETS, ADOLF, SWEETS

"It was white sugar, that's what did it," said the handsome woman sitting on the chair next to mine at the Jazz de Milo. I was out drinking again, but of course there was no chance of my becoming an alcoholic because I was drinking only to find myself, and because I was a little depressed. It was temporary—really.

This woman was also well into her stemware, having thus far consumed the better part of a litre of Vouvray that cost only slightly more than my car payment. She opposed refined foods, she said, which was ironic considering the price of linguini in this particular establishment.

"It was sweets, that's what caused it. 'Sweets, Adolf, sweets,'" she continued. "He would never have done those things if he hadn't been on white sugar."

"You mean everything Hitler did was caused because he ate white sugar?"

"He was an addict," she said. "Half the time he was so buzzed on sugar he didn't know what he was doing."

"So World War II was caused by . . ."

"White sugar." She leaned back, her point made, and hung her long arm over the back-rest of the revolving barstool. She had finally devastated me after a half-hour presentation on the evils of refined foods, conventional science, and especially white sugar, which was evil for everyone, particularly for people with "vulnerable chemistry."

"It really does make quite a lot of good sense," I told her, hoping my disingenuity would be covered by inebriation. Personally, I was convinced that Hitler had become a world-renowned madman because of toilet training. However, I attribute a lot of things to toilet training—probably because of my toilet training. I practiced restraint in my comments, operating on the assumption that tolerance was the best policy and that without it I would never see the inside of her kitchen cabinets. I couldn't resist one little point, though. "I heard he was a monorchid," I said. "I heard that had something to do with it."

My female acquaintance didn't answer in time to prevent the interruption by a man sitting on the other side of her at the bar. He had been trying his luck with her from time to time as she and I conversed, usually taking any opening to side with her.

This time he said, "He was no kind of orchid, friend. He may have been crazy, but he had balls the size of grapefruits."

I had heard this kind of comment before as an indication of admiration of masculinity, but all I could think was how uncomfortable any but the baggiest of fashions would be if it were true.

"Yes, I understand that," I said, though I didn't. "But I meant to say that regardless of size, he had only one grapefruit."

"You two are a couple of sexist bastards," said the woman, "if you think the size of testicles means anything."

I readjusted my position on the barstool. I felt as I often did in the presence of an attractive woman who could think—like I was in the company of a superior being from an alien planet, before whom I needed to cover the obvious defects in my evolution, and at the same time pretend I had no interest in intergalactic breeding. My competition, though of a lower order, perhaps hiding in his pants the remnants of some prehensile past, also realized this was a crossroads in continuing any relationship at all with the statuesque woman who had a medical degree and a bedside manner we both wanted to get to know.

"If you assholes knew anything," she continued, "you'd know that when a person's nutrition is balanced and all the poisons are removed from their system, they'll behave appropriately. Hitler did have a character disorder, but I'd bet if you looked into his early life you'd find the cause was diet." She downed her drink.

"Yes. Yes, I suppose you're right," I said thoughtfully. "I thought I had a point, but what you say makes a lot of sense." I ordered a Bloody Mary with extra celery. "I've been thinking about doing a fast myself." (Very slowly.) "I thought it might help to clear some of the crap out of my system." On the other hand I might just talk it out.

"Yeah? I could help you with that."

How—deny me food?

"You could? That would be great."

The guy on the other side of her gave up with this saccharine show of agreement and began a conversation with a fern sitting on the bar next to his drink. I wasn't surprised—it's still in vogue to speak with plants, though most people do so more rhetorically than our friend, who seemed likely to move in with it.

My medical friend and I continued our conversation. I did okay because I have a 45-credit major in science—not enough to get into the space program, but good enough for me to gossip about Einstein. She was

a new-age physician anyway, a disciple of natural heal-
ing, in which knowledge is not the most important in-
gredient.

Eventually we became friends from this beginning,
dated, and began spending our nights together. I was
dozing at her house one night when at about four a.m.
I was awakened by a scream that removed a quarter-inch
patch of tissue from my ear drum with the precision of
a laser. Just for the hell of it I screamed, too, and did a
half-gainer from the bed into a large closet, landing amid
a gaggle of high-heeled shoes. A full clothes bag fell on
top of me. I lay there quietly for fifteen minutes or so
just in case someone was looking for me. The screams
only lasted half that time, after which there was quite a
volume of silence.

Finally, I heard, "What the hell are you doing in the
closet?"

"Am I in the closet?"

"Yes. Are you all right?"

"I'm wearing too many shoes, but other than that,
yes."

"Well, come to bed."

"Are you going to scream anymore?"

"I'm sorry. I should have told you I do that. It's
primal scream."

"I have a heart condition."

"I won't do it anymore tonight. I only did it now
because I've had a bad experience with astral travel."

"Is that the travel agency near where you work?"

"No, dummy. It's out-of-body travel."

"I take it there's no drinking car."

"I don't usually travel when I'm sleeping with someone, but tonight I had a feeling it was coming on. When
I dozed off I came awake floating up there by the ceiling." She pointed to a spot at the foot of the bed. I lifted
my head from my resting place in the closet to see. "I
could see both of us sleeping. I had such a feeling of
peace."

So had I, no doubt, before the scream. I wondered
if I should ask her if I had continued my bad habit of
sleeping with my mouth open.

"I must have remembered just then that I was sleeping with you because suddenly I saw a blinding light and
a voice, the voice of my spiritual adviser. She said, 'He's
such a nebech!' "

"Are you Jewish?"

"No, but my spiritual advisor is."

"Oh."

"Then she showed me where I'd be in ten years if I
stayed with you."

"Where was that?"

"Somewhere in the suburbs," she said with disgust.
"My spiritual advisor showed me what the cabinets
would look like—we had Karo Syrup. I was feeding the
kids Chock vitamins to make up for the Wonder Bread
in their sandwiches. We had a picture of Annette Funi-

cello on the refrigerator. The scene my advisor showed me took place in the kitchen and you were talking about Carl 'ick' Sagan, and pouring Red Dye Number 40 onto your pancakes. That's when I woke and screamed."

"But you know I'm not like that," I said, "I've been on a fast for about two weeks. I eat all my granola in the morning. I've even stopped complaining about the food bill from the Sassy Rabbit Natural Foods Store. Why would you see me as a bad influence?"

"I don't think your feelings on the subject are genuine," she said, getting out of bed and putting on her robe. "I realized during the visit from my advisor something I've wondered about for weeks—the color of your aura, it's brown. Nobody who's healthy has a brown aura."

"I've had gastritis," I said weakly, but I knew it was no good. She had soon packed the few belongings I kept around her house and put them into my Nike bag. I added a pair of spike-heeled shoes I had become fond of during my stay in the closet. It was probably more evidence of dietary problems.

"If you clean out your diet, maybe we could see one another again," she told me at the door. "But you'd have to be awfully sincere to convince me."

She closed the door, leaving me standing on her porch in the semi-darkness, the only light being that from a passing burglar's flashlight. It was a good neighborhood during the daytime, but at this time, it seemed good to take up jogging. I soon made it to an all-night donut shop, but by that time I had lost a few dollars and my watch to an all-night mugger.

I sat there for several hours, thinking about my relationship with the good doctor and the sorry ending I had just witnessed. I had a sugar-coated, a cream-filled, and two jelly donuts and several times as dawn approached I thought about forming a political party—something with a military wing. I gave it up after discussing the subject with the female clerk who said Hitler had not been a sugar junkie after all, but a semi-vegetarian, a dietary purist.

"I don't believe in that stuff," said the waitress. "I like donuts." She snapped her gum and lit a cigarette.

"Me too," I told her. "Give me two more of the chocolate-covered and tell me where you go for dessert when you're not working."

CRIMINAL LOSSES

Usually I spend my Sunday evenings at the symphony with any of a dozen subscribers to the Smithso-
nian, but I decided that as a change of pace I would
spend this one behind a dumpster in the alley near the
First National Bank machine. There, I shared a bottle of
Mad Dog 20-20 with Mort, a denizen of those parts.
Mort was in his sixties and claimed that before alcohol
had overtaken him—it had been nipping at his heels for
years—he had been a fairly prominent and respected
criminal. Since his retirement, or as he put it, the Fall of
Man, Mort had pretty much given up crime, both for

ethical and practical reasons.

"Mainly, it don't pay," he said, wiping the bottle with a sleeve I would have kissed as reluctantly as his mouth. He passed the wine over to me as I asked for details of this rather trite, but no doubt well-supported thesis. He told me that "nowadays" things were just too different for him to keep up. He gave as an example his last "hit."

He said he had been given the job of "doing in" this labor leader who lived in the suburbs of Bloomingdale. The contract had arrived late in the day but before the end of business hours, and he needed the money, so he decided to go ahead with it, then stay in Bloomingdale and eat out for dinner—a sort of change of pace for him.

He got to the guy's house okay, and found the guy's front door unlocked and no one else in the house. When he scouted around he found His Nibs upstairs taking a bath—a good sign he thought since naked people are easier to intimidate.

"So there he is in the tub," said Mort, with an ironic smile that was easy to ascribe to age and alcohol since he was old and drunk. "I looked around for something to do him in with—pros almost never use a gun because household objects are much more dangerous—and I see there's this space heater on the rug.

"He barely had the chance to say, 'Who the hell are you?' before I picked it up and tossed it into his bath

water. You should have heard him shriek. I was already
figuring on calling in my pizza order—I always have this
craving for Italian food after a hit—when all of a sudden
the lights go out.

" 'Christ!' I hear this guy say, 'Not that circuit
breaker again. You can't run anything in this bathroom
without setting it off. Hand me that bathrobe!'

"Five minutes later I'm down in the basement throw-
ing circuit breakers while this guy is upstairs checking
the lights and using the phone. We got the power on
just before the police arrived. That cost me ten years in
Joliet—or was it La Jolla? I forget. You gonna hog that
bottle?"

I passed the wine and Mort sniffed the bouquet before imbibing. It was either his method of removing
nasal hair or enlarging the blood vessels in his nose.

"Another time," Mort blurted, dribbling wine on his
designer-label shirt, "I was on this burglary in St. Louis.
We stole their security system—it was worth thousands
of dollars—the whole system for this big house."

"Didn't you want their money?"

"Oh, sure, we took a few things, but the real
money's in these expensive security systems."

"Didn't it go off?"

"Oh, sure," he said, waving his hand to dismiss this
fact. "But nobody ever pays any attention to those
things. Nah, we got away clean. It was later we got into
trouble. We tried to sell it to someone and the Attorney

General arrested us for fraud and misrepresenta-
tion—hey, it was hard to beat that—two more years in
the slammer. That was the time I learned to make wine
from sugar, yeast, and dirty socks.

"So," said Mort, "I asked my boss for a transfer. I
figured I would spend a little time in white collar
crime—the work's clean and if I got caught I figured to
be incarcerated with the likes of John Mitchell or John
Dean, or some other clean John. Maybe I would get a
Presidential pardon—or at least an 'excuse me.'

"So I got put in charge of laundering some money
they skimmed off of gambling. I'd take this cash and use
it for down payments on houses—hundreds of houses
and apartments. Then we'd have all this property as col-
lateral for investment." Mort patted himself on the chest
in congratulation. "It was my plan," he said, "and it was
brilliant. My boss was very impressed.

"It would have worked too, but the guy I bought the
houses through didn't own them. I had all these con-
tracts and promises of deeds just about the same day he
got picked up by the Feds."

Mort spread his hands in a gesture of helplessness.
"What could I do? I didn't own the houses and I didn't
have the money. My boss was a pretty good guy, but
business is business. I figured I was in a tough spot."

"So what happened?"

"What do you mean, what happened? Are we talking in an alley and drinking formaldehyde, or am I hal-

lucinating?"

I nodded and shrugged. "So what happened to the other guy, the one who scammed you?"

Mort pointed across the alley at a white-haired man laying under a pile of newspapers and garbage. "That's him. I ran into him about a month after he got a suspended sentence. He just didn't have the heart for another run-in with the police, so he came down here."

"You didn't beat him up?"

"He had a bottle of wine," said Mort.

"Oh." I looked over at the white-haired man again, wondering if Mort was telling the truth—drunks can be so disingenuous.

I was thinking about sleep when Mort solved the problem by saying " 'Night," and bopping me over the head with the now-empty bottle.

When I woke the next morning I found my watch and wallet were missing, but I was a little more optimistic about Mort's chances of survival after that, figuring he hadn't entirely given up his career.

His streak of bad luck wasn't over, however, as I later discovered he had taken my keys, located my car, and stolen it.

It's a Pinto.

Good luck, Mort.

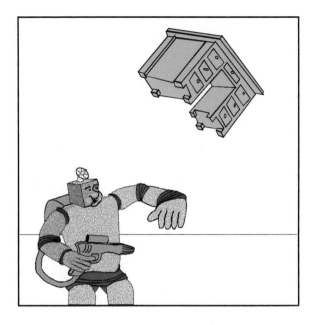

TIN SOLDIER
(No real hero ever dies)

For human beings reincarnation is at best a vague hope. If it occurs, the being in question never knows, never remembers who he or she was in the former life—except through the intervention of some seer, or psychic, or hypnotist. For cybernetic beings, however, reincarnation was a commonplace occurrence, though less metaphysical and with a more clearly defined creator.

For Seymour II, who was a cybernetic—not a robot, nor automaton, for he had some discretionary abilities and feelings—the creator and instrument of resurrection was a corporation called MHOTRON. MHOTRON was a war materiel supplier that had contracted to provide troops for an expeditionary force on its way to Alaska to restore order. Alaska had been something of a problem for the Administration for a number of years because the state was one of the last sources of fossil fuels within the national borders. Only twenty or so people still drove private automobiles—everyone else got around almost entirely by rumor—but these few were powerful and wanted to ensure a lifelong supply of unleaded and ethyl. When the Alaskans began making independence noises and then imported several thousand copies of the Koran, the Administration decided to intercede.

In fulfilling its contract with the Department of Defense, MHOTRON came across thousands of deactivated cybernetics whose CPUs and circuit boards lay gathering dust on the shelves of various repair shops and warehouses. MHOTRON decided they would suffice as combat troops and support personnel.

Seymour, who had lain inactive for a number of years, was lifted from the shelf, dusted, and checked out by technicians. For awhile he experienced a montage of memory from an earlier life as a short order cook for McDonalds, and by the time the memory had been erased, he had developed a certain dislike of fast food restaurants.

His new body was much taller and heavier than the one he remembered. He inquired about this and was told that the Army needed more ferocious-looking personnel than those required by McDonalds. He also had something of a problem at first, goose-stepping instead of marching, but this was corrected by replacing one of his PROMs—programmed in South America. His ethics PROMs were then jumper-bypassed to get around instructions regulating his behavior in human and cybernetic society. These ethics were based on rules dreamed up by the science fiction writer Isaac Asimov. Their content in detail is unimportant, but suffice to say, they prevented Seymour from firing machine guns.

After thorough testing Seymour was packed into Styrofoam and Bubble-Wrap for the trip to Alaska. He lay there, docile and expectant, as MHOTRON technicians switched him over to a mathematical mode intended to keep his circuits occupied during the flight (analogous to a businessman thinking you will be entertained by Muzak when the operator puts you on hold). Initially intrigued by the series of mathematical games, puzzles, and music, Seymour soon tired of them, and by the time he arrived in Anchorage, he loathed binary mathematics, whether or not it was the basis of his existence. Deep within him now dwelt a budding Luddite, and though polite and tractable because of programming, he bore a mild repugnance for all things mathematical and mechanical.

Whereas this was the future and people had had enough of the particularly brutal kind of wars common to the Twentieth Century, the weaponry had changed quite a bit, especially the arms given to the cybernetic mercenaries. The Nerf-like weapons they carried fired golf-ball-like objects guided by heat-seeking sensors and propelled by compressed air. These weapons had a surprising range, equivalent to conventional firearms, and when these projectiles struck humans in the chest they usually knocked them flat long enough for the cybernetics to overrun their defenses. The weapon was set to seek and strike any object within the temperature range of 90 to 103 degrees; and though they occasionally surprised a passing moose or polar bear, they usually struck an Alaskan citizen. Even on the occasions when the ammunition mistakenly sought out a hot drink like a coffee nudge or a hot-buttered rum the Alaskans were disheartened and suffered lowered morale.

The Alaskans were plucky and good marksmen, having practiced many hours on wild game, but had neither the sensors nor the tracking ability of the cybernetics, and they had not been fed tapes containing the entire military history of mankind. Toward the end of the brief war, by which time the Alaskans had run out of ammo for their rifles, they resorted to such tactics as building catapults and lofting anything they could find at the oncoming horde of cybernetic mercenaries. Desks were among the most available items among the Alaskans and were often launched at the mechanical soldiers. It was symptomatic of a major problem in the Alaskan ranks—too much reliance on hard-copy documentation. Occasionally during the fighting a human being was damaged more than Seymour's forces had intended and there was a great hue and cry in the media. But it was not lost on Seymour that no such outcry was forthcoming when one of the cybernetics was damaged by a falling desk or struck in the CPU by an enemy bullet. They were simply allowed to lie where they fell, alarm lights blinking monotonously like signs outside a cheap hotel.

Unlike their opponents, however, few of Seymour's comrades were permanently deactivated, although some, for a lack of spare parts, suffered the loss of limbs or certain sensory abilities. After the war these were either rehabilitated or mustered out to while away their days on the streets of Anchorage begging for nickel-cadmium and lithium batteries.

When the hostilities had ceased—they lasted only a few months—the cybernetics were given a choice of returning to the Lower Forty-eight or remaining in Alaska, available for easy recall.

Seymour, who had retained a certain dislike of machinery, proposed to spend his days as a government forester. He took a Thoreau module—designed for Alaskan servants before the war—staked out a small acreage, built a cabin, and gathered around him a few animals. He eventually learned to feed and care for his charges, though he was surprised by the absence in them of any kind of self-diagnostic programming.

He subsisted on reconditioned batteries, tended to most of his medical complaints himself, and saved others for the occasional passing repairman. He developed a number of hobbies, chief among them poetry. His work appeared in several national magazines and eventually prompted a young woman who was the poet laureate of the state of California to come and live nearby in a cabin she constructed. He accepted her company, but soon learned she required a diet more varied than rabbit pellets and barley, and was no more fond of electrical shock than the animals. She did have self-diagnostics, however, and she was always telling him what was wrong with her. On the other hand he could never figure out anything to do about it.

COMRADE WOMAN

Tom was having lunch with a new woman friend
when she stabbed him in the lapel with her salad fork
and said, "Men have to stop treating women brutally,
with no consideration for their rights."
He quickly agreed, and she withdrew the fork as
Thousand-Island oozed from the wound in his jacket
and a shard of Romaine fell dead in his lap. He resumed
his meal, attacking his *L'Eggs Almondine* with more
than the usual vigor, as his friend entertained him with
an anecdote about "this damned Tom cat" that had
been hanging around her house bothering the female

felines. She had enlisted the aid of a friend to capture him and take him to the vet where his enthusiasm for the opposite sex was surgically dampened. Her apparent satisfaction with the outcome of this episode was too much for Tom's comfort. He ate mostly in silence, nodding from time to time in agreement, wondering how he could disassociate himself from "men" without losing some of the perks thereby associated—especially the ones the neighborhood cat had just relinquished. Try though he might to ignore it, Tom was irritated that all during this repast the waitress had been slow and a bit rude, and had once, inadvertently he was sure, poured coffee on his crotch. As they were standing to leave, he made a mildly peevish remark about this, and said the tip would be smaller than usual and paid in *escudos* for good measure.

"You have no right to judge one of my sisters," said his companion, looking around for a salad fork. Finding none, she evidently decided that using his tie as a garrote would suffice as a substitute measure. "If she had been treated equally she wouldn't have to grovel here—she could be an executive or a lawyer."

It seemed pointless to mention how much groveling is required of executives or lawyers, or that if anyone had groveled recently it had been him, hoping to prevent more scalding of sensitive tissues. He could have also mentioned that although he had a master's degree in comparative liturgy he was currently selling display advertising on the side doors of Volkswagens.

At her door later she seemed surprised when he declined her offer of a drink. He told her, quite honestly,
that he was tired, but didn't bother to mention that his
sleepiness had brought on the fear that surgical tools
and local anesthetic were perhaps hidden near the in-
cense and could too easily be brought into play during
an inadvertent nap.

Granted, this woman was more than usually militant
in her feminism (she was recently arrested for imperson-
ating a Teamster), but, nonetheless, he tried over the
following several weeks to convince her she was
confusing *this* with *that, him* with *them.* He told her the
grade school analogy about the grains of sand on a
beach, apparently identical, but in truth like snowflakes,
absolutely unique (though don't expect to tell one from
the other at a Stanford-UCLA game). He told her he
deserved to be treated as an individual, that, though he
had been raised "as a man" (except during the brief, dis-
orienting period when his parents told him he was a
crustacean), he was gentler than most. He admitted to
having a man's prejudices and problems except as other
more enlightened sexes with different viewpoints had
made inroads, or in the more persistent cases, dents.

But Billie seemed unconvinced. He did his best to
demonstrate that he thought of her as an equal and tried
to treat her like a man. He borrowed her tool set and
didn't return it, beat her at tennis and bragged about it

in a bar, then later in the week applied for her job and slept with one of her girlfriends. She tried to be game and respond in kind by attempting to run over his dog and later fired a rifle bullet through his living room window.

Still, things weren't right between them. Soon enough the inevitable happened—they had trouble in bed. It began because he tried to break his stereotypical male behavior, and instead of remaining relatively quiet and stoic throughout coitus, began shrieking when he reached orgasm. Her response, besides slapping him on the face, was to say, "The one place I expect you to be manly is in bed."

So he sat up and turned on the football game. Which he happened to hate. Within minutes he was asleep while she was on the phone to her bookie.

That is when the well known Buddhist principle of cause and effect took over.

Their nightly tension reliever was interrupted, which was inconvenient as he had committed all his nights to her in an effort to "work on the relationship" and share ideas. Now, during these evenings, he watched TV as she sat in the corner thumbing through *Playgirl.* Since he had recently agreed to avoid *Playboy* except during haircuts, he could not play this game tit for tat. The best he could do was peruse *National Geographic,* though never pausing too long at pictures of tribal natives.

Nights they lay in the dark and entertained themselves separately—he by seeing how labored he could make his breathing, she by doing her best to imitate Absolute Zero on the Kelvin scale.

After four days he was developing frostbite, so he sent her an interoffice memo requesting a conference. After she had read the minutes of their previous meeting, he made his case.

"I'm not sure I believe in this anymore, Honey," he told her, with as much concern, honesty, and equality as he could demonstrate on a face as capable of tragedy as Mickey Mouse. "I'm having a crisis of conscience. I'm not sure I believe in these values anymore. Maybe we could just relax. I'd like to be spontaneous, breathe perfume again, look at a woman and think she has a nice—"

"—Don't say it, buster," she warned. "Just *don't* say it. That really puts me off. It's just a phase you're going through. In a few days it'll pass. It won't help you to go looking for another woman—*every* woman wants the respect I do. *Every* woman wants what I want—some of them just don't know they want it."

"But, what *do* you want?"

"Well, if you have to ask, there's just no point telling you."

And she broke up the meeting to go mist the plants and change the oil in the Volvo. Naturally, with all this going on, it seemed a good evening to drink, and by the time it was dark he found himself sitting on the edge of a sharp-edged couch in an apartment in the University District, exchanging compliments with a 22-year-old zoologist whose concentration on the lives of non-neocortal mammals had left the seeds of feminism not merely unharvested, but virtually unplanted. Her acceptance of his minor lapses from respectability—like when he reached over playfully and patted her thigh—gave him a very warm feeling for her, which the warmth and elasticity of her skin did not dispel. Soon he was seeing her on the side—actually as a dietetic main course, since his relationship with Billie had lapsed entirely. When Billie announced her interest in a muscular stock broker (or perhaps it was stock boy—he wasn't listening well in his euphoria), it seemed an auspicious time to tell Wendy he would move in with her.

After several weeks of contentment, a time you would remember because there was a regional shortage of coconut butter, fatigue and doubts set in.

Wendy was so accepting and even-tempered that he became a bit bored. When he told her it was unnecessary for her to cook every night, or mentioned that she didn't have to fold his socks, she didn't seem to know what he was talking about. He picked up a few of the standard books on the subject of feminism and encouraged her to read them, feeling she would surely become more interesting when she became more enlightened.

They worked out a division of household duties which seemed less traditional, and she taught him something about cooking, though this was difficult since she didn't know much. He gave her lessons on how to tune up a car and how to be aggressive in traffic. Things began to perk up and they had nightly discussions about their progress. In the early fall she joined a women's support group and both of them were pleased and excited the first night she left the house, entirely on her own, to seek out her identity with other enlightened women.

He waited for her that night—one, two, three a.m. passed without a word from her. Finally, at about four she came in, a bit disheveled and smelling of several popular nonprescription drugs. She undressed in the dark as he lay in bed, quiet, trying not to cause trouble or be upset, but feeling very hurt and slightly tremulous.

As she climbed into bed, quite casually and without regard for the disturbance it might cause him, he said, "Wendy, Honey, are you okay?"

"I'm okay," she said, "Go to sleep."

"I don't think I could go to sleep, Hon, I'm worried about you."

"Don't call me 'Hon,'" she said forcefully. "Call me 'comrade.'"

He turned onto his back and stared at the ceiling. This equality thing was making him very tense.

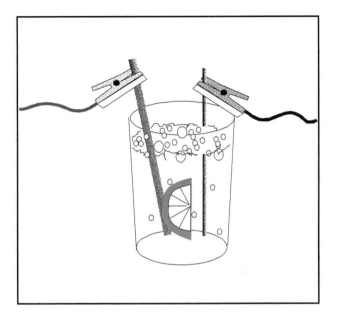

SOCIAL SCIENCE

Blake smiled the secure and beatific smile of the true believer. We were standing in the center of Tin Tung, a country-western Chinese restaurant. The owner, John Wayne Wong, was belting out a bad version of "Ring of Fire" from the stage. The restaurant was full of middle-aged people attending a singles dance. Although I am not middle-aged, I was present as a concession to my therapist, who wants me to spend more time with people of my own generation.

Blake and I had withdrawn from the crowd of girdles

and hairpieces, Birkenstocks and mood rings, in favor of more philosophical, even scientific conversation.

Blake was selling the concept of cold fusion.

Now, the dispute over cold versus hot fusion was several years old. At one time physicists had assured us that they would be able to generate energy by fusing atoms instead of splitting them, but that this would take billions of dollars and be decades in development. All of a sudden some chemists from Utah claimed they could go the physicists one better and produce fusion in a laboratory beaker for about the price of your average movie. This made the physicists mad, there was a war, and now the chemists were viewed by mainstream science with about the same respect as Dan Quayle entered in a spelling bee.

"I thought cold fusion was proven wrong," I interjected before he could get very far into his lecture.

"No, no," he said, waving his hands in easy dismissal. Blake was well into middle-age, but still styled himself as a 1960s hippie. His frizzy, graying hair was pulled back in a ponytail and his black suit sported bell bottoms. As a concession to our surroundings, I guess, he wore a bolo tie over a white shirt. His heavy, horn-rimmed glasses were a warning of the possibility of serious intellectual pursuit. The delighted smile currently displayed appeared most often on his bearded face when he was discounting the ideas of conventional science. "They *think* they proved it wrong, but the *way* they did the experiment was the mistake. That made it easier for the physicists to get them."

Blake had been pitching his idea most of the evening. Now he was selling the idea to me, but I wasn't ready to buy. I was waiting for some young woman to stumble, confused and lost, into this crowd. For my money she could even be a physicist.

"But I heard it didn't work," I said. "They read the results wrong and it turned out they hadn't produced as much energy as they'd put into the experiment."

"They just chose the wrong materials," said Blake. "I've discovered that the original experiment used the wrong metals. I use metals no one ever thought of. My reaction creates much more energy."

Now, I had spoken with Blake a number of times and never thought of him as someone who had test tubes and Bunsen burners in his apartment. I had imagined his laboratory as a well funded, but technically casual institution that resided in his head and always produced favorable results.

But he proved me wrong.

"It works like this," he said. "You just put a metal as a cathode and an anode into certain liquids—so that you have a cell . . . your gin and tonic will do." He pulled a pair of metal rods from his pocket and dropped them into my drink. A pair of wires ran from the rods. "I have a battery in my pocket that provides the power to fuel the reaction," he told me.

I looked down at my drink, which was now frothing slightly. This only occasionally happens when I order a well drink.

"I have discovered," said Blake, watching my drink with some satisfaction, "that fusion not only works, but works when applied to any number of different compounds—though cocktails are among the best. It also causes reactions in most types of yogurt, some fruit drinks, and also some chili recipes."

The drink was beginning to vibrate in my hand and I had given up any idea of finishing it. The people around us had so far taken no notice of the steam rising from our location or the look of horror on my face.

"That's interesting, Blake," I said, trying not to sound alarmed. "Is this going to taint my drink in any way?" I thought he would take the hint and remove the rods.

"Oh, it'll heat it a little bit, and your drink will contain traces of deuterium and tritium; though, as a side effect it will also have a slightly higher alcohol content." He seemed in no hurry to remove the rods. "One gin and tonic about this size will provide enough power for your house for a month—of course, you have to have it in the proper receptacle to deliver the power."

"What happens if it's in a drink?"

"There's really no danger as long as you don't leave it in the drink for more than about five minutes."

"Then what?"

"Oh, a small explosion—possibly," he said cheerily.

"Why don't you finish my drink," I said, handing it over.

"I've already had one too many," he protested, trying to return it, and not succeeding. I pretended to have lost muscular control over my hands.

"I'll say one thing for you, Blake, you've got to be the only person at this dance selling cold fusion."

"Oh, *no*," he said, his brows narrowing with concern that I should think him anomalous or an oddball. He was struggling to hold the drink and remove the rods. "*Dan*'s around here somewhere."

At that moment we heard the thump of a small explosion and a shriek from across the room. Steam spread out in a fog from the source.

"He's over there!" Blake said excitedly, pleased that his partner in fusion wasn't shirking his duties.

I took this brief distraction to move away before my drink contributed to the entertainment.

I walked to the quietest edge of the dance floor I could find and ordered several new, not-so-explosive drinks from a waitress. Shortly afterward, standing at the edge of the dance floor, I discovered in myself a new conviviality. I had a non-threatening drink, good companions, and a higher alcohol level due to two shots of Stoli.

An attractive woman near me caught my eye.

"Hello," I said.

"Hi," she answered.

"How are you this evening?"

"I'm fine, what about you?"

"I'm okay now. I had a narrow escape from cold fusion earlier, but I've recovered."

"Oh, you met Blake. He's a character. I'm afraid he's a little too scientific for me."

"You prefer a *less* scientific approach?"

"I'm a psychic," she said.

"Oh."

"I know people think psychics are kind of kooky, but I'm not one of these psychic-reading types. I work with the Information Superhighway—in a way. I recover lost documents."

"You what?"

"Recover lost documents." She smiled, "It's a little complicated. Have you ever read any Carl Jung?"

"When I was *young*-er."

"Well, I've discovered a little-known side effect to his theories. You see, he believed in the collective unconscious. What I've discovered is that all our unrecovered word processing and database files go there. I'm sure if you've worked with computers you've heard the phrase 'alphabet heaven.' "

"Yesss . . . ?"

"Well, it's a real place. I get in touch with it and recover the files."

"You mean you're able to get documents back?"

"Well, I haven't done that yet, but I've gotten frag-ments. And I provide a lot of comfort to the people who have lost their documents—I mean it's very painful for people to lose their work. We talk about it and they grieve. Sometimes if conditions are right we're able to get parts of the files back. They let me touch the disk, and they concentrate. I sit at the computer and wait. Sometimes I get whole paragraphs. If I don't get any-thing through the Ether, they can still dictate to me—either way it's twenty bucks an hour."

"*I've* lost a couple of documents."

"Everybody has."

"Actually I lost a document just tonight—before I came to the dance. I was writing a love letter."

"Oh. To your girl friend."

"No, no. I don't have a girl friend. I just get bored—you know how it is being single. Maybe you could look at my disk."

"Sure." She handed me her card. It read: *Shirley's Psychic Document Recovery. No Document is Ever Really Gone.*

"What about right now? This is kind of a boring dance."

"All right."

As we were walking through the door I heard a shriek as another patron's drink fell victim to Blake's electrodes.

There was no guarantee I would recover my documents, but it was certainly a better risk than ordering another gin and tonic while Blake was in the room.

DOWNTIME FOR BONZO
(The De-evolution of an Intelligent Machine)

A man may wish for the quiet life, and many do. For a cybernetic, such a wish was ironic as it did not spring fully formed as some intrinsic desire for freedom and fulfillment. Even the slightest wish was merely the result of some geeky afterthought on the part of the software engineer. Beliefs and feelings formed through experience were mild compared to firmware that determined basic values and attitudes. Seymour's designer had lived in the suburbs of San Francisco and learned about nature through a freshman-year reading of Thoreau's *Walden*, the more ironic for Thoreau's poor understanding of the natural world. As a result of programming by this engineer, Seymour had retired from the army to spend years in Alaska wielding a woodsman's axe and living in a cabin.

He had gathered around him a few animals and one human, a woman named Desireé. She was once the Poet Laureate of the State of California though she had lost her title as punishment for living in Alaska.

Seymour might have remained a millenium with these creatures and this woman, assuming a sufficient supply of spare parts for all concerned. But one morning Seymour booted up to learn that the news on all the COM lines was of a new war.

Federal conscription for cybernetics began, which for Seymour meant a certain return to service in the army as one more inventory item in that collection of silicon and metal misfits. Most draftees were kludged versions of cybernetic individuals who had lived earlier lives in careers such as fast food, dry cleaning, and construction. This not only meant that Seymour would be a target for bullets and shells, but there would be evenings spent listening as some former cybernetic drywaller from Milwaukee explained how to tape Sheetrock.

Seymour was as patriotic as the next cybernetic, but battle and an accidental exposure to magnetic radiation had lessened his enthusiasm for repetitive warfare in which nothing seemed to be permanently settled. In the human community in years past such attitudes were less of a problem because of a natural human forgetfulness, and also, if enough time passed, a new generation would inherit each new war. Cybernetic memories were too reliable for this technique and their lives too long. Getting out of Alaska to avoid this military fate was not going to be easy. He had registered with the government. They had his address and knew his checksum.

For the first time since arriving, unannounced and uninvited, from Orange County, his neighbor, Desireé, came in handy. She traveled by snowmobile to Sitka and paid for counterfeit papers that showed her as his owner, indicated his place of manufacture as California, and declared his purpose as farm laborer. Giving her reason for leaving Alaska as concern for her safety, De-sireé was able to gain passage for herself and "Juan" on a space-available military flight, and hours later Seymour stepper-motored out of the baggage compartment of a jumbo jet at the San Diego airport.

The price Desireé exacted from him for his escape was not high by his standards, but seemed to satisfy her reasons for seeking him out in the first place—she wanted to learn his method of writing poetry. She was nonplussed when, after having traveled all that way from Alaska and having gone to the trouble of finding him a place to live, he told her that poetry was simply a byproduct of internal algorithms that provided him the ability to employ integral calculus to avoid objects lobbed at him from enemy positions. Perhaps the source of his method was the reason critics raved about the wonderful "elliptical" quality of his verse.

In spite of her disappointment, Desireé remained his friend and enrolled in night school hoping to learn enough about calculus that she could write a poem using his method.

As a result of his association with Desireé, Seymour fell in with a strange crowd, mostly actors, and mostly human beings. Having already been identified as a poet, he took only a short step down in becoming an actor.

However, problems remained. His stature drew attention and increased the threat that his draft status would be discovered. Desireé had an idea. She introduced him to an agent who suggested he try for a part in a remake of an early 1950's comedy called *Bedtime for Bonzo*. The story was about a college professor involved with a precocious chimpanzee. In the remake, *Downtime for Bonzo*, the chimp was to be replaced by a household robot. These robots were chimp-like—typically not too intelligent, but cute and affectionate and capable of climbing to all the hard-to-clean areas inside and outside the house. The agent told him that to qualify for the part he would be completely rebuilt in the image of these chimp-like machines. This would solve his problem with the draft.

"But I don't want to look like a chimp," said

Seymour.

"I'm your agent," his agent said, "and I know best."
So Seymour allowed it to be done. He could be
independent at times, but had basically been programmed to be agreeable.

Once the reconstruction was complete, getting the
part was a snap, since he was so much more versatile
than any of the typical household robots. He could at
one moment impersonate a chimpanzee's amusing gate,
and the next quote Shakespeare. The director not only
chose Seymour, but had the script revised to favor his
intelligence and versatility.

His new role brought mixed results from Seymour's
point of view. The image he saw in the mirror was in
conflict with his programmed self-image and the
accompanying pride in that image he had once felt.
This didn't improve even when the movie was released
and he became a star. It was of some comfort that a
number of cybernetic female groupies didn't care that he
was short.

But Seymour was not a happy cybernetic. He had
wanted to escape the draft, but had imagined returning
to his forest someday—and he hadn't planned to return
as a chimpanzee. He wondered what he could do about
it and began to read Hollywood histories for a clue to
possible improvements in his career. Perhaps when the
war was over he could change his image and return to
his former shape.

But after a week of reading biographies, Seymour asked Desireé to summon a psychological technician to administer the digital equivalent of Prozac.

The literature had not been good. There was the superhero who had become typecast and, despite his immortality, had managed to shoot himself. There were the actors who got pigeon-holed as second bananas and played them until they got brown spots. There were the starlets who played sluts in their very first roles and never got out of the gutter. Cowboys ended their Hollywood careers riding on wooden horses in front of paintings.

A chimp was going to be a chimp. War, or no war, it appeared he would have to remain this short creature living in a big house.

Seymour was more disconsolate in his present role than in any of his previous lives. It had not been a problem being a short-order cook with a fairly normal body and a simple but dignified role. His life as a soldier had been odd, but at least not embarrassing, and had led to a most safisfying life as a woodsman in Alaska.

In his present life he was a freak. He was adored by humans for being cute and clever. He was adored by certain cybernetics for being successful. He was adored by some females of both groups for being a star.

But he was a freak to all of them and most of all to himself.

He was nearly thirty-five years old. He was just over three feet tall and referred to affectionately in the press as "Bonzo." His given name, Seymour, had been an homage to a major contributor to the development of the computer. It was not flattering to have this name replaced by that of a chimpanzee. Further, the studio insisted he be put to bed by a nurse at eight o'clock in the evening.

Under these circumstances his next action was inevitable.

He began robbing banks.

Bank robbery in California was easy for cybernetics. They used their understanding of bank machines to get account information, and after less than a minute emptied the account at a cash machine. The bank security system could quickly detect the bogus transaction through a characteristic cybernetic fingerprint so the cybernetic's next concern was a quick getaway.

The traditional getaway—by automobile—was complicated. The decline in the number of cars had recently reversed, but the new cars were very different from their ancestors. For one thing their engines were so tiny they were rated in rabbitpower. And, more significantly, cars had undergone a digital revolution and were now equipped with brains and feelings.

But owners of the new cars were less than thrilled with the cars' personalities. They discovered that the software engineers had instilled in their creations the same narcissism and vanity that pervaded their advertised images. Someone on the development team had decided it would be "cute" and "poetic." This resulted in vehicles that had their own emotional and social needs. Cars pursued personal agendas. They went to body shops and ordered cosmetic alterations. They had their grillwork modified. They had themselves re-painted. They reupholstered their interiors, often with garish velours and shag rugs. Cars had their tires changed just to perk themselves up.

Some owners got so tired of this that they sold their cars and didn't replace them. Mass transit actually became popular. There became such a glut on the market that some cars couldn't find an owner and had to get along on their own. A culture of homeless cars developed. They were often seen in groups in Safeway parking lots, or parked along the beach, or crowded in gravel pits in areas outside the city. It was difficult to do anything about them because they could get away pretty easily and the police had to use cars to round them up—cars that didn't like the idea of bringing in their own kind.

And many homeless cars were willing to pair up with cybernetic bank robbers. The robber could acquire the cash, and the car could get away. The robber would get the money. The car would get an owner—someone to love them and praise them and pay for expensive changes to their appearance. Or so they thought, for the robbers often had no intention of honoring promises to the cars. They planned a getaway from the bank, followed by a getaway from the car.

But this was where complications could also set in for the robbers. Getting away from a car was more difficult than getting away from the bank. Some unscrupulous cars had their own plans and left the robber in an alley with tire-marks on his tattered torso.

Others found that emotionally dependent cars were hard to shake. And this was bad, because it could provide a lead to the police.

This is how Seymour was foiled.

His bank robbery scheme was an effort to get his own money so he could pay for reconstruction. As a cybernetic, he couldn't legally own any substantial property. Seymour didn't even have a car as it was illegal for a cybernetic to own another cybernetic, except sometimes for tax purposes.

So he formed a casual alliance with a car, a homeless Subaru. He would have been all right had not the little car, suffering a form of adolescent hero worship, become so attached it could not bear to part company.

Soon the studio and the police were aware that he was being followed by a homeless Subaru that was wanted for a string of bank robberies. They connected the two, and it wasn't long before they discovered money in one of Seymour's hollow legs.

Ironically the bank robbery incident improved the range of roles available to him. All charges were dropped and he was offered parts far outside his original range. He played lead in drama and comedy, action and romance.

But his agent continued to refuse to allow a change in his shape or the basically cute and affectionate nature of his public image. His agent told Seymour it would ruin both their careers to make any such changes.

Seymour continued to be distraught by the difference between his mind and its aspirations. He was upset by the appearance of his body and the image it projected. He made it known that running away to some forested wilderness was not beyond his programming.

Unbeknownst to him, his agent had arranged to resolve the difference for him. One night during Seymour's downtime, a cybernetic version of a lobotomy was performed. After that, Seymour was so content being a chimp that he couldn't have imagined being anything else. He could dance around and hop from shoulder to shoulder with the best of them. And a part of his firmware dreams were fulfilled, for he spent his days in the wilderness now, though it was usually more of a jungle than a New England pond. His new level of intelligence left him only qualified for this type of picture, and he actually seldom noticed that he was in a movie set. This fate wasn't exactly the kind of bucolic existence that Seymour's software designer had imagined, but later in the year the designer's dream and Seymour's present did merge somewhat, when the studio starred him in a feature titled, *On Walden Pond with Tarzan and Jane.*

Acknowledgements

I'd like to thank Pete Delaney for editing this book. I'd also like to express thanks to Kate Armstrong, Barbara Blumenstein, Brook Blumenstein, Lucille Berentsen, Garth Hitchens, and Margaret Petrone for their support and help in preparing the manuscript.

The Author

Has been this way for as long as anyone can remember.

Order Form

OffByOne Press
9594 1st Ave NE #322
Seattle, WA 98115-2012

Send me *Clueless In Seattle* for $10.95

Name_____

Address_____

_____ZIP_____

Washingtonians add 8.2% sales tax
(Add $3 per book for shipping.)